I0542569

"This is exactly the kind of book I look for—literature with a soul. Adolescents and young adults will be entertained and enlightened; educated and inspired. The Tale of Aynil the Traveler is one parents will want to read with their children, just so they can hear the stories too. Viva la fairies!"

Angela Engel

Parent, Educator, and Author of *Seeds of Tomorrow; Solutions for Improving our Children's Education*

"Paul Rodriguez has created a fairy tale in a style that is different from the norm. He takes a simple idea and breathes depth into his characters and mystery into the adventure to make the reader think in new directions. Perfect for the reluctant reader, the story is easy to read yet still has complexity. This is a fairy story that even boys will like!"

Katherine Dockerty

Middle School Librarian, Westminster, CO

"Rodriguez tells wonderful lies to reveal the truth. The two most important words about this book: I believe"

Tom Van Steenhoven

Author of *Billy Books, The Moon Adventure*

TALES OF FAIRIES

The Tale of AYNIL THE Traveler

This novel is a work of fiction. Names, characters, places and incidents either are the product of the author's imagination or are used fictitiously. Any resemblance to actual persons, living or dead, events or locales is entirely coincidental. Any person claiming otherwise is just plain silly.

© 2011 by Paul Rodriguez

All rights reserved. No part of this book may be reproduced or transmitted by any means, electronic or mechanical, including photocopying, recording, or by any information storage and retrieval system, without the express written consent of the Publisher, except where permitted by law. For information address: Renaissance Peak, Arvada Colorado.

ISBN: 0-9843281-2-3, 978-0-9843281-2-2

Printed in the United States of America

Cover Design by Deborah Miller

TALES OF FAIRIES

The Tale of AYNIL the Traveler

By Paul Vincent Rodriguez

Renaissance Peak

through the light and the night and the dust in the air
through the smiles and tears and hope and despair
fly the magicians and storytellers "on the wing" as they must
that are the fairy and the traveler inside each of us

Special Thanks to:
My family and friends who also believe.
My children who inspire me every day.
Joshua Bixler and Celestino Rodriguez
who had to leave us so that we might learn.
Steve Brown whose portrayal of a tooth fairy
in training inspired this character.
And, as always,
the fairies who trusted me with their stories.

The Tale of
The Tales of Fairies

It was late summer 2006 when I happened on a very rare occurrence. It was a fairy demotion. I watched as Qwendaline dropped her wings, bowed her head and grew from eighteen inches tall to almost six feet. She was now a human. Needless to say I was not supposed to see this but there I was among one hundred or so fairies of all types who now had to figure out what to do with me.

After overcoming the shock and fear of a human wandering in on their ceremony, they accepted me as a friend. Fairies are a very spiritual group. They believe that everything happens for a reason and that I must have a special purpose to have shown up during such a rare event. When they discovered I was a writer, they began telling me their stories.

Some told their stories reluctantly while others never seemed to stop talking. Every story was unique and carried a great message. Some of these stories helped me through difficult times in my own life. The story telling went on for months. About a year and a half after I met the fairies, I arrived at the clearing to find the entire group waiting for me. It was not another demotion. I stood nervously as the entire group fluttered up to my eye level and Qwendaline's mother, Grace, approached.

"You must go do your job now," she said softly.

"Am I no longer welcome here?" I asked.

"You are always welcome. But you have a job to do. The stories we have shared were not only for you. It is time to share them with others."

These are the Tales of Fairies as told to me by my friends in the clearing. Some stories are action packed while others are more cerebral. Some are about boys and some are about girls. I have tried to keep them short—like I said, some fairies tend to ramble—while maintaining the messages each thought important enough to share. I hope you enjoy reading the stories as much as I enjoyed hearing them.

Aynil's Defining Moment

Sometimes Aynil wished his parents had been more involved in his life, made more suggestions, guided him away from some bad elements; you know, told him what to do.

You see Aynil was not what you would call a smart fairy. Intelligent, yes, he scored highest in his class on the F-A-Ts (Fairy Aptitude Tests) and would have been valedictorian had it not been for that catnip incident in grade ten. Catnip is strictly forbidden because it brings, well, cats into our environment. Cats will eat anything they get their paws on and once they get all nipped up you don't know what they'll do.

Aynil and his parents were best friends. They always treated him like a grown-up and he treated them like kids so none of them really had any responsibilities. His parents were both products of the Nineteen-Sixties when the world was a safer place; not as safe as the Nineteen-Fifties but still safer than today. Television was in black and white and all three stations went off the air after midnight.

Aynil first realized his family was different when he was six and came home from school with homework. He thought his life was over.

"When am I supposed to play if I have to do school work at home?" he asked. He was, as they said in the Sixties, bummed. So his dad took the homework, threw it in the trash can and said, "go play."

"What the heck?!" the young Aynil exclaimed with a smile.

Aynil flew up a couple branches and told his best friend, a very cute girl fairy named Flaylen, what his father had just done while he helped her finish the math questions he no longer had to do. The next day he had to stay in for recess for not turning in his homework and got double the questions that night. Now he was *really* bummed. So his father threw that homework in the trash can.

"What the heck?!" the young Aynil exclaimed again but with more concern. He dove into the trash head first to retrieve his assignment before it got that night's apricot nectar all over it. The work took about ten minutes to finish because, like I said, he was intelligent, and he again went up to help Flaylen finish hers.

That's how life was for Aynil. If he didn't like something he didn't have to do it or eat it or deal with it in any way shape or form if he didn't want to. IT STUNK!

CHAPTER ONE

A Unique Name

My name is Aynil. The Ay sounds like "I". I've had to explain that to everyone all my life. That is why I hated the name for most of it, my life that is. Aynil is an acronym for All You Need Is Love. My parents loved The Beatles. What a surprise. I am the only child of Barden, my father, and Joylyn, my mother, whom I called Barden and Joylyn, per their request. It wouldn't be so weird now that I am almost fifty-years-old but it definitely turned some parents' heads when I was in elementary school.

My father is a woodland fairy. It is seasonal work which gives him time to work on his novel. He has been writing it now for forty years and thinks he is nearing completion of his first draft. It is approximately twenty-thousand fairy pages which is substantially less in human pages because fairy novels are written one word to a page.

The size of the books alone requires great strength just to lift them. It is the primary reason fairies prefer haiku poetry over other forms of literature.

Joylyn, or "Mom" if you must, continues to be the primary money earner of the family and has been a fairy godmother for as long as I can remember. Fairy godparent is one of the sweetest gigs you can get because of the tips. Inevitably, the person you are watching over wishes for something nice for you as a token of their appreciation. Of course the things they think are nice don't always translate into nice here. For instance, one time a little girl gave Joylyn a kitty. Kitties tend to chase and sometimes eat things that fly. Fortunately, she was able to make the kitty a kitten and left her as a gift for another human family who loved it very much.

But like I said, I'm older now. I consider myself lucky that both my parents are still around. My father wrote his novel and I am in training to become a tooth fairy. To be honest I don't know if I like the idea of trading money for something that came out of a human's mouth. But the pay is decent and I've come to appreciate working nights. That's how I came to be here when Qwendaline was demoted. That's something I don't think I will see again for a very long time. But I wasn't always a tooth fairy, as you might have guessed; otherwise why would I be in training? No, at first I was a traveler fairy.

I was seventeen, soon to be eighteen, when I graduated from high school. It was 1981 and disco was still popular. Our class song was "Imagine" by the human John Lennon who had been killed the previous winter. I have come to realize that even humans have occasional moments of extreme clarity. He is also partly responsible for my name because he was one of the Beatles whose song I am named from.

I watched the twenty-six members of my class flutter single-file through the rite-of-passage hole in the tree trunk of the old cottonwood and come out the other side looking noticeably different. Even Larnish, the class clown, emerged contemplative. It was said that the moments inside the old cottonwood would reveal the secrets of life that fairies needed to know to successfully fulfill their destinies. What would those secrets be for me? I thought of the words my father and mother had repeated over and over throughout my life.

"Don't limit yourself to one set of wings. Experience the world. Be life. Attempt everything. Have no regrets."

One beat at a time, I kept rhythm with the rest of my classmates trying not to let my temporary wings catch in the surrounding leaves, or worse, in the flowing blond hair of Flaylen who had grown into the most beautiful fairy in our class. Up ahead, my classmates and friends each emerged with their first set of shiny, new, adult wings. Some wings had the chameleon qualities of the woodland fairy. Others were the dramatic and ornate wings that define those mature enough to be someone's fairy godparent. There was no mistaking the sleek, aerodynamic design of the exclusive mischief fairies and tooth fairies. Those wings were limited to fairies fit and agile enough for those jobs and willing to endure the extensive training curriculums.

The inside of the tree was pitch black even though it was a sunny day and there were giant holes on both sides. I had flown through the tree a number of times playing touch-and-go with my friends as a child and never remembered it being dark. But this was graduation day.

Flaylen looked over her shoulder and smiled. I smiled back. With some friends, smiles are all you need. She disappeared into the darkness and reappeared on the other side with, what else, the matching blond wings of a fairy godmother. Her face, her smile, however, seemed unchanged. It was as if she already had all the knowledge the tree would present her before she entered. It was perfect. Everything was perfect. And it was my turn to go in.

CHAPTER TWO

My Destiny

*A*s with every important event in my life, I entered into this rite of passage with excitement and trepidation. All my life I looked forward to the day I would graduate high school and begin my life as an adult. Now I stood motionless, staring at a dark hole in a tree that seemed to speak my name. One last glance back to the crowd. I saw my parents. They stood with one arm around each other waiting for the moment when I would decide to go in. Their smiles were peaceful and reassuring and they were the last things I saw before I entered.

Although I didn't see it, I'm certain my entrance into and exit out of the great cottonwood were anything but graceful. The sensation of breaking through the energy plane made me jerk my arm back. But instead of my arm coming back, the rest of my body was pulled in.

It was dark. Really dark. Can't-see-your-hand-in-front-of-your-face dark. But it was peaceful. The first thing that happens is you reflect on all of the important moments in your life; like the first day I came home from school with homework, the fight I got into last year with Nargan, the school bully, and the time I stole five packs of berry beads from the candy store and got caught. Then the voice of the great cottonwood said four things:

"Wherever you go, there you are."

"Wherever you are, be there."

"Whenever you leave, go."

"Always remember your name."

The next thing I knew I was being unceremoniously bounced out the other side with a brain full of questions. What did that mean? Wherever you are, be there? Where else would I be? I was so confused and distracted that it took a few seconds before I heard the loud cheers from the crowd that were reserved for the rarest of all fairy wings; those of the traveler.

My mind flashed back to my vision of Barden and Joylyn telling me of the travels of Carlin, the greatest traveler of all. Carlin was noted to have had more experiences than any other traveler and could tell stories from dusk till dawn without repeating a single sentence. He would tell of places where fairies spoke different languages and others where they didn't live in trees. He told of riding on flying machines and eating unique foods. Their faces glowed as they spoke of Carlin and his bravery and his memory and his life. The more they talked about Carlin, the more I wanted to be him. I wanted my parents to speak of me with such high praise. I wanted their eyes to light up and their chests to sigh when they thought about me. So when I was asked at the end of each school year what I wanted to be when I graduated, I confidently stated "I want to be like Carlin. I want to be a traveler." Now that I was him, I realized I might never see my family again.

Traveler fairies come once every twenty years or so and serve as the colony's link to the outside world. While there are many jobs to do, most fairies stay within five or ten kilometers of their homes. They will come in contact with fairies from other colonies but seldomly do they see or hear about the far away places the traveler sees. The colony has two traveler fairies; one currently sharing their stories and another who is out on his travels or "on the wing" as we say. The awarding of the wings of the traveler not only means that the colony will have new experiences to share in a few years but that they will soon be reliving vicariously the experiences of the current traveler who will be returning. And so, the crowd cheered.

I looked back to see the dirty and stained burlap wings that would fly me thousands of miles. Not as stylish as I expected. My parents smiled and applauded as those around them offered thanks and congratulations. My classmates who had gone through the mighty cottonwood cheered. Those classmates still to come cheered. Even Flaylen stood before me and applauded. And while everyone in the colony celebrated our great fortune, I wondered what I had gotten myself into.

CHAPTER THREE

Every Journey Begins With One Flap of the Wings

The graduation party lasted late into the night with classmates talking about who got wings they had asked for and who didn't and how those who didn't get what they asked for, after some thought, realized that the wings they did get really were better. I spent most of the time saying "I don't know" to the questions the others were asking about where I would go and what I might see. I really didn't know how this was supposed to work.

The next morning I woke to the sounds of banging and crashing associated with party preparations. A band warmed up in a corner of the clearing and wings flapped rapidly among those preparing food and other entertainment. Barden entered my room carrying a slim, camouflage frontpack.

"Good morning?" he questioned.

"I think so," I replied.

Barden crouched at the foot of the bed. He handed me the frontpack.

"It's bullet proof, just in case. The camouflage should give you extra cover when you need it."

I had forgotten the number of Carlin's stories that included being shot at by humans. Again I wondered what I had gotten myself into.

"Looks like quite a party down there," I said.

"Yes. Too bad it's not for you," Barden answered. "Well, it's sort of for you. Your mother and I will think it's for you, but everyone else will be awaiting the arrival of Tappin." Tappin was the last traveler fairy to leave our colony. He could not return until I left.

The party started in the morning as kind of a brunch with a nice buffet and some light music. The families milled about going from table to table delivering any gifts they felt I absolutely needed. Being on the wing is like being a hobo; you don't take much with you. The party wouldn't reach full strength until I was no longer visible. They did this to protect the feelings of the new traveler. They didn't want it to seem like a "good riddance" celebration. I didn't really care. All I knew was I was having lots of food with lots of maple syrup on it.

Once in full swing, the party continued until Tappin touched down and his wings fell off demonstrating his intent to stay. This can take hours or even days depending on the returning fairy's desire to stay. Once you have been on the wing, it's hard to let go of the freedom. But eventually every traveler succumbs to their obligations to the community and drops his or her wings.

Joylyn walked in carrying a pair of cargo pants and a camera vest.

"They have lots of pockets," she said and she began to cry.

"Hey, isn't this what you always wanted?" I tried to comfort her. "I will see great things. I will meet new people. Maybe I'll write a book about the experiences."

"I will miss you. You are my only child and I may never see you again. I am putting my hair pin in this pocket where it can protect your heart. I hope some day you will care enough for someone to remove the shield and give it to them."

It was at that time that I realized why they had wanted me to call them by their first names all my life. They knew I was going to be a traveler the day I was born. However impersonal, calling them by their first names all this time did not make my leaving any easier.

Barden, Joylyn and I sat at the table closest to the buffet as is customary for the new traveler. Friends and family members came to visit and offer words of advice based on hearsay and rumors they had heard about travelers. Others just brought more food from the buffet as it was pretty much the only thing anyone could give me since I would be traveling very lightly.

Then Flaylen floated in. Flaylen always floated. I wanted to reach into my breast pocket and give her the hair pin Joylyn had just given me but knew that it was inappropriate considering how long I might be gone.

"Are you ready?" she asked.

"I don't know."

"Are you scared?"

"I don't know."

"Are you certain this is what you really want?"

"There's only one thing that I am certain I really want," I replied. I took a long look at her glowing face.

"I will always be here," she said.

We had only that moment to remember each other's faces before the Mayor called out "The wind is up! It is a great day for flying!" The crowd roared and began chanting my name.

"That's your cue," said Barden as he helped me rise. "Did you get enough to eat?"

"I think more than enough."

Barden led me toward the high stump in the colony where everyone had gathered. "You can't be too careful," he said as he stuffed muffins and dinner rolls into my pockets. "Even stale bread has nourishment. Remember your horticulture lessons and don't eat anything that's not poisonous to humans. Not at first anyway. And stay away from yellow snow," continued Barden.

"Don't forget to write in your journal when you get the chance," chimed in Joylyn. "And write like humans, not fairies, and your pages will last longer."

The crowd parted as we got closer. Barden helped me secure my front pack tightening the strap across my lower back and under my lower rudder wings. The crowd of well-wishers closed in behind us as we passed.

"Stay in the trees as much as possible and avoid the cities if you can," he said.

"I'll do my best."
When we had reached the high stump, he faced me and held me by the shoulders.

"I hope I see you again. Oh, the stories you will tell," he said.

"Finish your novel. We will tell stories to each other when I get back," I answered.

I gave Barden a great hug and with two flaps of my wings, lit lightly beside the mayor on the top of the high stump.

"It is with great pride and anticipation that we say goodbye to our newest traveler," the Mayor began. "Aynil, we have watched you grow and marveled at your terrific memory. We know you will bring us great stories of the outside that will fill our minds with vibrant color and great adventure. We wish you good winds and safety on your journey."

The crowd turned its attention to me. I had nothing to say. I just smiled and looked into the faces of those I would be leaving behind. What would change? Who would change? And who would I tell my stories to when I returned?

Flaylen. Flaylen would always be here. I looked once more at her smiling face, closed my eyes, and darted straight up into the sky. I was a traveler.

CHAPTER FOUR

Garland and
the Golden Tassel

The fog lay heavy like a comforting blanket over the Iowa corn. The corn tassels limped over with the weight of the heavy air and the moisture it brought. It was night time and the headlights of the speeding cars and semi-trucks on Interstate 80 glowed and floated like gigantic fireflies only to disappear behind a hill or the bridge that crossed over the freeway at the Little Amana exit.

A row of poplar trees rose toward the sky about a half mile from the Interstate and served as a wind break for the corn it protected. The trees stretched thirty feet into the air; none so ostentatious as to make themselves taller than the others except one. That is where we were settling in for dinner after a long day of detasseling corn.

Detasseling is when you cut the top off the corn stalk. It stops the plants from cross pollinating and creating mixed strains of corn. It is one of the few jobs fairies can do during the day. The corn offers cover from humans and the remote nature of farming keeps the average Joe away.

I was taken in by the Harris family and kept under cover while my wings morphed into the shape and color of those who worked the corn. You see, we traveler fairies aren't always accepted by those who choose to stay in the same place all of their lives. And while I enjoyed my time on the wing, there were times I found myself jealous of those who knew what they wanted and were happy to build a life where they were. Garland wasn't one of them.

Garland and I met abruptly in the field when we both attempted to detassel the same stalk. He came at the tassel with a vigor I had not seen in any of the other fairies. Swooping in from ten rows away, his blade nicked my hand as he scalped the top of the tall green plant. He dove toward the earth with his prize and lit gently on the ground beside where I had fallen. He gazed with great wonder and anticipation at the silky strands, closed his eyes and turned the tassel upside down. His face glimmered with hope but that faded the instant his eyes opened.

"Looking for something?" I asked sucking on my cut hand.

"Cut yourself did you?" he replied too distracted to hear my question.

"I think you did this."

"I think I'd remember taking a cut at a co-worker."

"I had my hand atop that stalk you just trimmed," I insisted.

"This one?" He motioned to the one beside us. "Oh. Sorry."

Garland was large in fairy terms. He was almost two-feet-tall and portly but unusually fast and nimble for a large fairy. Pretty accurate with a tassel blade too. Less talented fairies would have taken my hand off at the speed he was traveling.

"I'll be okay," I replied.

"You should have someone take a look at it to be sure."

I held my hand out to allow Garland to examine the wound.

"Not me," cowered Garland. "I hate the sight of blood. Makes me want to hurl. Go see the nurse or a doctor or something."

"It's not bleeding anymore."

"What's that liquidy stuff?"

"Spit."

"Apparently spit makes me want to hurl too. Just take it somewhere else."

I wiped my hand off on my shirt and offered him my other hand to shake.

"Aynil," I introduced myself.

"Aynil? That's a weird name. I'm Garland," he returned and grasped my hand firmly for a moment. "You new here?"

"It's temporary."

"Temporary? You're a traveler, aren't you? Hey, have you seen anything good? Seen anything interesting?" Garland was exuberant with his questioning to say the least.

"Not really. This is my first stop."

"Oh," said the disappointed fairy.

"What's so special about that tassel?" I asked.

"Nothing, as it turns out. I thought it was the golden one."

"The golden what?"

"The Golden Tassel. You don't know about the Golden Tassel? Everyone knows about the golden tassel. Every year the great fairy Iowa plants one corn stalk in each of the large fields that has a golden tassel," explained Garland. "The fairy that finds it is granted one wish; anything they want."

"Garland?!" A gruff voice rained down from above. It was Garland's father, Trunk. One glimpse and I could tell where Garland got his size.

"Garland. What are you two sittin' there for? We have five rows to finish today."

"Aynil got a cut on his hand," reported Garland.

"Did you have someone look at it?"

"It's not bad. I'll be fine," I replied.

"Then let's get back to work. Sunlight's a'wastin'."

Garland tossed the non-golden tassel to the ground and flew off to trim the tops of more corn stalks. I picked the discarded tassel from the soil and tucked it into my vest pocket opposite my mother's hair pin. Golden or not, it was the reason I had met Garland and that was important to me.

CHAPTER FIVE

Advice From
A Fellow Traveler

Over the next months Garland and I became great friends. He told me stories he had heard from other traveler fairies that passed through and, since I really didn't have any stories to share, I listened.

One evening, when the work of detasseling was done, there was a banquet for all of the fairy groups working the corn fields in the area. The lines for food were long and everyone was especially hungry after finishing multiple rows of corn. As a guest, I tried not to take too much food or even be so forward as to be one of the first in line. It's kind of an unwritten creed amongst traveler fairies since these fairies are also sharing their lives with us.

Garland was making the most of the gathering by showing off his strength to the many young females. He did this by lifting each female over his head until they pleaded for him to put them down. Then the females would flutter off giggling to their girlfriends who they would then send over to be lifted in the air by Garland. I never remembered the girls in my colony being that silly; especially not Flaylen. I wondered how she was doing.

I reached the front of the food line where it seemed everyone's mother was standing with an enormous spoon behind a huge dish or pot ready to scoop the largest portion of food you have ever seen onto your plate. And everything smelled great. There was cornbread, creamed corn, corn stuffing, corned beef, and my favorite, bread pudding.

"Quite a spread," said the stranger next to me.

"It's amazing."

I looked beside me to see something I hadn't seen since graduation; the stained burlap colored wings of another traveler fairy. He was much older at approximately forty-years-old.

"I'm Abe," he said.

"Nice to meet you. I'm Aynil."

"Aynil?"

"It's an acronym. All You Need Is Love."

"Mine too. Another Boy, Ethel. Ethel was my mom. She already had six boys. I was number seven. My dad wanted a girl," explained Abe. "Mind if I sit with you?"

"If we can find a place."

"Follow me."

I followed him to the farthest end of the table passing the occasional group that would offer a disapproving glare to Abe who always replied with a smile.

"Some people don't like our kind," said Abe.

"You can tell I'm a traveler too?"

"Everyone can tell if they know where to look. Your roots never change."

"I don't dye my hair," I replied bewildered.

"Your wing rods have roots that attach to your spine. The roots are different based on where you're from. You can't hide where you're from...nor should you ever want to."

I began looking at the roots of the fairies around me. Abe was right. I hadn't noticed this before.

"It's how we travelers find each other."

"Are there a lot of us?"

"In some places. This is a fairly common stop. Most farm fairies are more accepting because they need the extra help we provide. They'd never get all these fields done without some outside help."

"How many are travelers?"

"Here? I'd say about twenty percent. Most of us will be leaving soon."

"Where are you going?" I said.

"Who knows? Home, I hope."

"Home? You seem pretty young to be done with your travels."

"I said I hope," he replied. "I'm definitely done here."

"How do you know when to leave?"

"You feel it in your bones. We call it 'getting pulled.' It's like some magical force is literally pulling you to the north or the east or some direction. Sometimes it pulls so hard you feel like every bone in your body will snap if you don't leave."

"Are you getting pulled right now?" I asked.

"Actually I'm dragging. I should have left a couple days ago but I've been fightin' it. Never know when you'll get another meal like this. I'll be leaving tomorrow. How about you?"

"I'm not leaving yet," I said.

"Guess you weren't here to detassel corn."

"Why else would I be here?"

"I don't know. All I know is wherever you go, there you are."

I flashed back to the cottonwood tree at graduation and the first message I was given.

"What exactly does that mean?" I asked.

"Everything happens for a reason," began Abe. "You were brought here to do something specific. You will be pulled when you learn what you need to learn."

"Learn? I'm just supposed to have experiences and tell stories."

Abe nodded as if he had heard this before. He put down his fork and wiped his mouth. I guessed what he was about to say was important since he barely bothered to stop chewing when he spoke before. He gathered his thoughts, took two sips of juice, and spoke.

"The biggest misconception about us travelers is that we are just tossed into situations for no particular reason. That we are sent off with no direction to have random experiences. The truth is, we are teachers. We teach by telling stories. The lessons we learn on our travels are those that are important to us and to our colonies."

Abe continued talking about something that I never heard because my mind was now filling with questions that no one could answer. Why was I here? How long would I have to stay? Where would I go next? What lessons did I personally need to learn before going home? What lessons did I have to learn for the colony before going home? And worst of all, how long would all this take? Carlin, the greatest traveler of all, had been gone for fifty years. Tappin, who returned when I left, had been gone for only thirteen years. Thirteen years would make me thirty-one when I returned. I would be young enough to start a family and maybe try something different like woodland fairy or some other seasonal position. I thought I could even handle fifteen or even maybe twenty years of traveling, I would have to think hard about having a family at twenty years. But fifty years?! Fifty would be the end of me. I would have to dedicate my entire life to this one endeavor. I would have to forsake all other hopes and dreams of ever having a family of my own, of ever seeing my mother and father, and maybe, of ever seeing Flaylen again. I couldn't bear that. I couldn't bear any of that.

"Only when we have learned what is needed will we be sent home," Abe continued.

"I can't do this for fifty years!" I abruptly interrupted.

Abe stopped talking. He knew I hadn't been listening. He picked up his fork and began eating again. Slowly this time. He didn't look at me. He didn't say a word but you could tell his mind was working. With three scrapes of his fork he cleared his plate. When he had swallowed his last bite, he again cleaned his lips with his napkin then laid it on the empty plate. He drank from his glass of juice to clear his mouth.

"There is only one Carlin," he said as he calmly set his glass back upon the table.

"You know about Carlin?" I asked.

"Everyone knows about Carlin. You're pretty new to this, aren't you?"

"This is my first stop."

"Ahhh, I understand," he said and made himself more comfortable. "How can I help? Do you have any questions?"

People always ask you things like "do you have any questions" at the worst possible time. It's either when you have been listening to them talk for an hour and you don't want to hear their voice anymore and on top of that you have to go to the bathroom worse than any time you can remember or you haven't been exposed to something, like being a traveler, long enough to develop any good questions. In this case it was the latter.

"No," I said. Fortunately for me, Abe knew better.

"How about I just share some things I have learned and you can ask questions as they come up?"

Abe went on to tell me about blending in and handling conflicts. He emphasized staying healthy and avoiding fights and shared a story of a traveler who broke a wing in a fight and was eaten by cats. He later confessed it was an urban legend and was probably not true. After hours of listening and two plates of food, I finally had a question worth asking.

"Have you ever lied to the other fairies?"

This threw him for a loop. Never in all of his stories had he mentioned a situation in which he did anything that wasn't noble or at least honest.

"Why would I ever have to do that?" he calmly replied. "We who travel bring very few possessions with us while on the wing. We have some clothes and some food and very little currency. But one thing we have unlimited space for is knowledge and experience. We bring with us everything we have learned on our travels and those memories and lessons are more valuable to us than any physical item. One thing I learned before becoming a traveler was to be honest. My parents would say 'Always tell the truth. Fairies can always handle the truth.' Now the truth will sometimes get you in trouble but it will also earn you respect for not lying to avoid that trouble. There were many times I was put in positions where lying was the easier way out but I stuck to my parent's motto and paid whatever price. I watched others take the other route and sometimes suffer greater in the end. I will not lie to you, some of them got away with it, too. The risk and decision will be yours when the time comes. But me, I never lied. Always tell the truth. The single most important thing I learned in my life and I learned it at home."

CHAPTER SIX

A Great Desire to Travel

That night I laid in my hammock looking at the stars on a clear summer night and thinking about everything Abe had said. I wished for him a safe trip and hoped that trip would be home. Some of the other fairies joked and danced late into the night while some of the more serious argued about the human political climate and what ethanol meant to the future of detasseling corn. I was about to drift off to sleep when I thought I felt a tug on my back. I wondered if this was the pulling sensation Abe had talked about. I felt the tug again but this time it was accompanied by someone whispering my name. Abe had not mentioned being called by name. It tugged even harder.

"Aynil. You awake?" Garland whispered. "Aynil?"

"What?!" I yawned angrily.

"That was some party, huh?" Garland mused.

"You woke me up to talk about the party?"

"I asked if you were awake. Did you see that tammy I was with?"

A tammy is a pretty girl fairy. Like any other label of "hot" or "cute," tammy is totally subjective.

"Which one?" I asked.

"The one I was holding over my head."

"Again I ask, which one?"

"The red-haired one. The one I held over my head for like two minutes."

I was still confused.

"The one I was dancing with the most," Garland gasped.

"I didn't see you dancing with anyone," I explained.

"Then you missed out. She was...she was almost perfect, she was."

"Almost?"

"Perfect doesn't exist in women, does it now?" he proclaimed.

I had not told him about Flaylen.

"I mean you're never going to find a tammy that takes care of you like your mother, are you? And isn't that what we all want?"

"That's what I hear," I replied.

"That's what I hear, too," he said. "So if you didn't see any dancing, you must have been way in the back. Were you eating by yourself?"

"No."

"Who were you with?"

"Just another fairy."

I tried to be coy and not give up too much information but Garland was not dumb.

"It was another traveler, wasn't it? A traveler like you, huh?"

"He's more experienced," I replied.

"Did he have any good stories? Did he tell you any secrets? Was he just getting here or was he leaving?"

"He's leaving tomorrow."

"You travelers are so lucky," said Garland. "How cool it must be to have no commitments and need no excuses. To just come and go as you please. To experience the tastes and sounds and smells of distant places and compare them to those you've already tried. To feel the pull of the universe letting you know it's time for a new adventure and to have no idea where the next one will be. Wherever you go, there you are."

"It's not as cool as it sounds," I contested. "I worry about getting hurt or sick with no family around to help. I think about the uncertainty of not knowing where I'm going or for how long? Sure, wherever you go there you are until the time comes when you are pulled away again. There is no rhyme or reason to why you go where you go. It's just to have another experience to go back and tell someone about. I have planned for this all my life and I am still scared for myself."

"Well I think it's cool," he said. "We don't have any travelers in our colony."

"You don't have travelers?"

"No one thinks we need them. Fairies like you come 'round here every year with your tales of the far off. What do you think everyone is doing down there right now? Listening to traveler fairy stories is what." He let out a frustrated sigh. "You know what the problem is?"

"Traveler fairies?" I answered the rhetorical question.

"No. It's this colony. They're all so stuck in their ways. They think that everyone born here wants to stay here. Some of us aren't so happy to listen to other fairies' stories. When I finally get that golden tassel, I'm going to wish to be a traveler fairy."

Garland yawned and assumed the position I had so enjoyed prior to his arrival, asleep in his hammock, while I lay awake looking at the stars and trying to figure out why I was here. The stars had no answers.

CHAPTER SEVEN

A Controlled Burn

*I*t was late August and I was still in Iowa. The detasseling season was long over and there was little for me to do other than gather food for winter and wait to be pulled. I watched from the high branches as the younger fairies were dressed and sent off to school. Garland would start his last year having once again been eluded by the Golden Tassel.

The families scurried around the dry brush and weeds that sprouted amongst the trees. To the south lay acres of broken and brown corn stalks left to be tilled under after graciously surrendering their ears to feed a nation of humans and a colony of fairies.

Further down the road, the dust cloud of a speeding pick-up truck inched closer and closer. The children off to school, none of us fretted the approaching human. We watched with curiosity as the vehicle neared the end of the road which stopped at the highway. The truck skidded to a dusty halt. The human paused to let the dust cloud blow past before climbing out and slamming the old, metal door.

The human reached over the side of the truck bed and removed a large propane torch. He looked frustrated as he removed an electronic device from his pocket, pushed some buttons, and spoke.

"Where is that fire truck? There's no wind right now and what breeze we do have is blowing to the north. This isn't going to last forever. I'm gettin' started now."

With that, the human lit the torch and began what is called a "controlled burn" that would clear many of the noxious weeds and grasses growing along the road and highway. He lit a few areas of brush on fire which began burning toward the highway just as planned. The flames grew gradually and moved slowly, always moving north. Wind was negligible and the smoke blew away from us and across the sparsely populated interstate. But this was Iowa and it was August and the temperature was ninety-three degrees. And this was Iowa, and it was August, and what was a gentle southern breeze changed abruptly into a steady northern wind with consistent heavy gusts. And, because this was Iowa, and it was August, what had started as a carefully planned controlled burn, quickly shifted directions and became a raging brush fire engulfing everything in its path. And in its path was the row of trees we called home.

The human grabbed his electronic device and yelled instructions that were incomprehensible over the roar of the wild blaze. The flames no longer crept. They jumped. They shot. They flew from source to fuel as a paper clip is drawn to a strong magnet. From my perch I could see what the other fairies suspected.

"Fire!" I yelled. "Get out! The fire is coming this way!"

I gathered my few belongings, my front pack and my camera vest, and swooped down to help as many families as I could as they gathered their important belongings. Through the smoke I saw the red flashing lights of a human fire truck. In the distance there appeared another. It no longer mattered because the tree closest to the road, the lead tree in the wind break, the first in the mile long row of trees that were our homes, was on fire and the humans knew there was no stopping it.

The fire trucks rushed away toward the nearest highway exit and the pick-up truck spun around and darted toward the house across the field of brown and broken corn stalks. At the house I saw another fire truck but it was not moving. It would stay to protect the human home while ours would be lost one tree at a time. Amongst the chaos, a powerful but calm voice called my name from above.

"Aynil," called Trunk. "Do you have your things?"

"Yes."

"I need you to get the children to the river."

"What river?" In all the time I had spent here I had never seen a river.

"Garland will show you. Tell him that we have his things and are hiding them for now. We will meet you all at the river as soon as we can."

"Where are they?" I yelled.

"At the school. Now go!" Trunk hollered back.

"But where is the school?" I returned but he was gone.

With that, I jetted down the row of trees. I had gone nearly half of a mile and had found nothing. I stopped and turned to go back but was distracted by the view of the destruction of the homes of my friends. The flames had now reached the corn stalks. The speed at which they raced through the field seemed as if everything was soaked in gasoline. Around the human house the three red fire trucks sat with water flowing from their hoses. They drenched the ground surrounding the human house. Smoke and ash blanketed the wind break.

I heard a loud coughing from behind me a moment before I was sent tumbling to the ground by what seemed to be a train. I looked up to see Garland darting through the smoke toward the largest of the trees that was now fully engulfed in flames. I flew as fast as I could and grasped his pant leg before he zoomed into the inferno.

"Don't go in there!" I yelled.

"My parents!"

"They've left. They're hiding your things. Your dad told me to take the kids to the river and wait. Where is the river?"

Garland fluttered amongst the remaining trees mesmerized by the wall of flames that would soon replace the green leaves with red, yellow and blue fire.

"Garland, it's burning too fast," I shouted. Garland was still mesmerized. I spun him around to face me. "Garland," I shouted again, "where is the river?!"

He glanced over his shoulder once more at the fire. "Follow me," he hollered and darted back in the direction we had come.

CHAPTER EIGHT

The End of a Colony

arland, dragging three kindergarteners, guided a strand of children age six to sixteen through branches and over bushes toward a thick cluster of trees in the distance. I brought up the rear dragging two preschoolers of my own. The grove was old growth with small trees hugging the large ones. The branches intertwined with one another making a thicket impenetrable by any land-based creature larger than a rabbit. But we were flying.

In unison, the strand of fairies rose up over the branches and instantly dove down toward the river below. The teenage fairies thought nothing of making light of the situation by dragging their toes across the top of the river creating tiny wakes in the water. We rushed toward a covered clearing on the opposite side of the water and lit on the banks of the river.

"Is everyone here?" I called out.

I did not claim to know every child in the colony. I could not confirm on my own who was there and who might be lost. I looked to Garland for help but he was mesmerized by the distant sight of the destruction of his home.

"Can everyone account for someone? Everyone, make sure your friends are here. Look around. Is anyone missing?" I jumped in front of Garland. "How many should there be?"

"What?" a dazed Garland answered.

"How many kids in the school?"

"Fifty I think."

I shouted to the children. "Everyone stay in line." No one did. I began counting anyway. "Please, everyone stay in line while I get a count," I shouted still to no avail. Twelve, thirteen, fourteen. The line began to divide into clusters. "Please, everyone, just stay in line for another minute."

"Get in line and be quiet!" boomed the instructions from Garland.

The area was instantly silent. Garland glared back at the crowd that re-formed its line almost instantly. I counted quickly. Forty-seven, forty-eight, forty-nine and Garland made fifty.

"I think they're all here." I told Garland. "Someone should tell them what's going on."

Garland took one more look over his shoulder at the fire that moved closer. He looked up to a blue sky with the occasional white cloud above. Then he looked at the other children who now looked to him for answers.

"The colony is on fire," he started bluntly. "Your parents have gone to hide your belongings and will pick you up here soon."

"How soon?" asked one of the older boys.

"I don't know," answered Garland. "By tomorrow I suppose."

"Are we going to be safe?" followed a girl of similar age.

"The river is safe," he explained. "If the fire gets too close or threatens to jump the river, we can hide under the bridge or cross under the highway to the north."

"Where will we go?" asked another of the teenagers.

Where would we go? Where would I go? I was a visitor. I had no home or family. How would I stay here? Am I supposed to stay here? Why haven't I been pulled? Am I supposed to go with one of the families or am I simply to go on the wing with no direction? Maybe I missed it and I was supposed to leave months ago. How could I miss a feeling like your bones wanting to snap? I know I didn't feel it. But why am I still here?

The teenager asked again more directly, "Garland, where will we go?" Garland had no answer. It was as if the enormity of the situation had finally hit him. He turned his wings to the group and spread them as wide as possible. He was no longer available.

It is interesting how some act in times of crisis. Those true leaders among us move quickly and precisely with no thought of how the tragedy will affect them. They seek out those in need and risk everything to help. Not until the storm has been weathered do they look back on what they've lost or forward to how their lives will change. Now that the children were safe, Garland's thoughts strayed to his family and his colony. He sat along the edge of the river watching the reflection of the fire in the water. He tossed a rock into the languid image when he saw me approaching.

"Everything will be different now," he said.

"Where will they all go?" I asked.

"They will find another field somewhere. Maybe Illinois. Maybe Nebraska."

"I've seen Nebraska."

"Exciting, huh?" he said sarcastically.

"'The good life' according to the sign at the border," I replied.

Garland smiled and rolled his eyes.

"Maybe you'll find your golden tassel there," I continued.

Garland sighed, then his wings flapped a giant beat and he rose. "The story doesn't say anything about the fairy Nebraska," he responded. "We'd better get back to the others. I hope their parents start showing up soon. I'm too young to be adopting kids."

CHAPTER NINE

Garland's Wish

arland and I and the forty-nine school children did what we were told to do; we waited. We waited as the smoke came closer causing us to dip shirts and rags into the water to use as filters over our faces. We waited as the winds died down and the fire trucks arrived stopping the fire just before it reached the river. We waited as the sun went down through a smoky horizon creating one of the most beautiful red and orange sunsets I have ever seen. And we waited as the youngest of the children curled up in our laps and fell asleep still asking when they could go home.

It was almost high moon when the first of the parents arrived for their children. A couple hours later we were saying good-bye to the last of them. Garland suggested each family stay here for the night but they all said they already had places to go. They each gave

Garland a great hug that reminded me of those I had received the day I started my travels. It reminded me of the items I had been given for my trip and especially my mother's hair clip. I pressed my hand against the breast pocket of my vest and confirmed I still had it. Then I pressed my other hand against the other pocket and felt the tassel I had saved from the day I met Garland. I pulled it out of the pocket and stared at it. What was once green was now golden brown. It was then that I felt it. A tingling sensation in my shin that was relieved briefly when I took a step to the east. When it returned a couple minutes later, I would again step to the east and it would go away. I was being pulled.

Garland finished the last of his good-byes and turned to see me holding that which he had sought all his life.

"You found the Golden Tassel!" he shouted.

"You found it. I just kept it," I answered.

"What?" he said.

"This is the tassel you almost killed me for..."

"I barely nicked your hand," Garland contested.

"I kept it," I explained.

"Why?" Garland asked.

"Because I thought it was special."

"Well I guess it is special, isn't it?" At first Garland looked dejected then he was resigned. "So, what are you going to wish for?" he asked.

"It's not mine to wish with. You found it."

"But you kept it. It's yours."

"I don't want it. I'm giving it to you."

"You can't do that."

"Why not?"

"Because you can't."

"Where in the story does it say the person who finds the Golden Tassel has to keep it?"

"It doesn't."

"Then here. Make a wish." I held the tassel out to Garland who refused to take it. "What's the matter, you afraid to take it?" I challenged.

"It's not mine."

"You saw it first."

"But it wasn't the one then."

"What wasn't the one when?" Trunk's large voice interrupted.

Garland and I didn't know it, but Trunk and Darla, Garland's mother, had been listening to our crazy argument.

"He's got the Golden Tassel," Garland blurted out.

Garland, realizing his parents were actually there, darted toward them and wrapped his arms around his mother.

"Did everyone get out all right?" Trunk asked.

"Yeah," said Garland. "The last ones left a few minutes ago. Where's everyone going?"

"We will be splitting up for awhile," answered Darla. "Some are going to Nebraska and Missouri but most are staying with family here in Iowa."

"What about us?" asked Garland.

"We haven't made any decisions," said Trunk. "We wanted to talk to you first."

"What about Aynil?" asked Garland.

One glimpse in my direction and Trunk knew about the tingling in my shin. "You're leaving pretty soon, aren't you?" he asked me.

"I think so. I think it's time," I replied.

"You're getting pulled?!" Garland's frustration showed.

"Don't be sad, sweetie. You'll make new friends," Darla said trying to calm her troubled son.

"Sad?! I'm not sad! I'm jealous!"

"Jealous?" asked Darla.

"I want to leave," proclaimed Garland. "I want to have adventures. Why don't we have travelers in our colony?"

"We don't have any travelers because no one volunteers for it," answered Trunk.

"Our people have always seen plenty of travelers," said Darla. "None ever wanted to endure what they go through." She looked over to me. "I hope I didn't ruin anything for you," she said apologetically.

I was too preoccupied with the tingling sensation in my leg to care.

"The life of a traveler is full of uncertainty," continued Darla. "You don't know where you are going or for how long. It can be lonely. It can be dangerous."

"I've heard seventeen years worth of stories from those passing through," said Garland. "I'm not afraid."

"But you will be gone for years. Carlin was gone for fifty," she said.

"I know," Garland said softly.

"That's what you really want?" asked Trunk. "You want to be a traveler?"

"Yes," said Garland.

"Then you should take that corn tassel from your friend. It might be the last thing you see of us." Little did Garland know just how right Trunk was.

The ceremony was small; Trunk, Darla and me. We celebrated Garland's early graduation from school and his traveler launch at the same time. It was my first experience with dragging as I fought the pull to leave with everything I had. It was the most painful experience I will ever remember. Garland accepted the Golden Tassel as a gift from me. Trunk and Darla had only hugs, kisses and words of advice to offer. Everything that wasn't necessary to sustain themselves had been burned in the fire.

With the ceremony over, I said my good-byes to Darla and wished Garland the best of adventures and hoped we would cross paths again. Trunk led me toward the edge of the river.

"Are you okay?" he asked.

"Yeah, I'm okay. I'm just dragging a little."

"Looks like it hurts."

"I wanted to be here."

"There's a part of me that always knew this day would come," Trunk said. "Anyone that spent as much time as he did looking for a golden corn tassel had to be unhappy with where he was. Thanks for helping him find it. I owe ya'." The last three words caught Garland's attention.

"Did you just call him 'Iowa'?" Garland asked.

Trunk looked lovingly at his son and said what he knew Garland needed to hear. He said "Yes."

An understanding smile rose on Garland's face. The story of the Golden Tassel had come true.

Garland went on to become the greatest traveler fairy ever. He roamed the earth and shared his stories until the extended age of seventy-seven without ever returning to the river or the colony that had been destroyed by the fire. Trunk and Darla lived "the good life" in Nebraska. Though they never saw their son again, they heard stories of him from other travelers that came through. The stories were so varied and so many that they knew he must be doing what he was meant to do.

I followed the tingling sensation in my leg and flew east. I had no idea how far I would go, I didn't know how long I would be there, and I didn't know why I needed to be there. But I did know one thing;

Wherever I went, there I would be.

CHAPTER TEN

Welcome to Motown

Traveling can be lonely and confounding. I was once sent to a cattail-filled marsh for the simple reason of hearing a red-winged blackbird sing. Although it was soothing, the sensation of being pulled to a place and then being pulled away from the same place in such a short amount of time was disconcerting. I assumed I was sent there to hear the bird's song but I was not pulled immediately after the song ended. I did not feel the pulling sensation until after the time I spent under a cherry tree.

I had begun collecting small mementoes from places I had travelled when I came across something worth keeping. Under the cherry tree I found a stick. Not just a stick but a whittled piece of cherry wood. It was solid and straight and felt as if it held the thoughts and frustrations of many hours of contemplation. From the shaping of the piece of wood came the answers to the many questions of its maker. It was a very special stick.

Anyway, as much as I enjoyed having moments like this to myself, I also enjoyed the company of others. As a traveler you are either alone or meeting new fairies–all the time looking for the message you were sent there to learn. The longer I traveled the worse this got because the longer I traveled the more I wanted to be home and the more I thought about Flaylen.

I took solace in the changing surroundings and noticed that the changing seasons offered more than just a way to mark the passing of time. It was my eighth autumn on the wing but each fall seemed to send me north. I stopped wondering why things like this happened about two years before. The red, orange and yellow oak and maple leaves looked like a forest fire raging below me. From the right angle, they even gave the impression of fire on the water of the lakes they bordered.

The area I was over now had lots of trees and lots of lakes. Lots of trees and lots of lakes usually means lots of bugs which I hated. I mean when flying. I hate bugs when I'm flying. They get in your eyes and up your nose and in your teeth if you don't keep your mouth closed. Normally I would just set down in the woods for the night and get some sleep. But tonight I was being pulled like never before and I did not have the energy to endure the pain of dragging another night.

I wanted to fly higher in the sky to avoid the bugs, but feared humans would see me. Because of my smaller size, I am usually confused with hawks or eagles although fairies don't glide as gracefully as those majestic birds. Nor do we eat small rodents or fish or other small mammals; at least not without cooking them first.

The trees and lakes kept coming even though the air began to lose its crispness. Smoke, dust and car exhaust now tainted the air. The only good thing about smoke and car exhaust is there are fewer bugs. I was near a highway and highways almost always meant cities and cities aren't easy places for fairies.

Cities are full of humans and most of the humans are what they call grown-ups. I think they call them grown-ups because they are all done growing up. Sometimes they don't stop growing out for many more years. Humans are like giants to us. Humans are usually three times bigger than fairies, in height anyway, and about ten times heavier. I once heard a story of a traveler who was sat on by a human. She was crushed; literally and figuratively. I heard it was worse than being caught by a cat. I can't imagine anything worse than a cat.

Below me was the highway. The highway became a freeway; humans call a highway in the city a freeway. Don't ask me why. Along the freeway were rows of gas stations and chain restaurants and motels and liquor stores and home improvement warehouses. The tires of the cars and trucks hummed along the asphalt. As I flew, the hum got louder and the cars and trucks got more plentiful. The freeway continued and so did the gas stations and the chain restaurants and office supply stores and mobile phone stores but there were fewer motels and small business buildings because the buildings were getting bigger. And the freeway continued and so did the gas stations and the restaurants and...

WHAM!!

The billboards. I forgot that freeways also have large outdoor advertising panels that stand tall in the grass and dirt along the pavement. The one I had just flown into was for an auto repair shop somewhere in the city of Detroit apparently. At least that's what the sign said. I looked like a dead bug on the windshield of the car in the advertisement. This was ironic since my face was pressed against a greater number of actual dead bugs that had also flown into the printed car's windshield with less luck than I had. The sticky bug juice from the unfortunate insects was like a paste keeping me from sliding down the sign. Pushing out with all the force my hands and arms could generate, I pried myself off the sign and dropped to the ground.

I wiped the bug guts from my face and steadied myself against a post as I stood up and surveyed the situation. The few clouds in the sky reflected the last hints of the red sun that was setting. It would be dark in a few hours and I still had not reached my destination because my shin was still aching. The headlights of the cars on the freeway began popping on. I would follow their path until I was pulled away.

I felt a twinge in my lower right rudder wing as I lifted off. I must have strained something when I hit the billboard. I could still fly without pain but my steering would be a little slower until I healed fully. I was in the air and moving as quickly as I could. The buildings got bigger, the gas stations and restaurants got fewer and the home improvement warehouses disappeared. I was in what the humans call downtown. And I was scared.

Downtown is not a good place for fairies. First of all, most grown-up humans don't believe in fairies and downtown is mostly filled with grown-up humans. The other thing that downtown has a lot of is, you guessed it, cats. I kicked the wings into overdrive. If I had to go through downtown to get to where I was headed, I wanted to do it quickly.

Then I heard it. Music. At the same time I heard the music, the pain in my leg had shifted telling me I had passed my destination. As much as I didn't want to be in the city, I had to turn back and follow the music. There was a strong bass drum with a rhythm guitar and a bass guitar. Typical rock and roll collection. But there were also trumpets and saxophones. And then I heard a voice say "I, can turn a gray sky blue." And another lower voice sang "I can make it rain, whenever I want it to." And yet another in a higher pitch sang," I can build a castle from a single grain of sand." And the last sang "I can make a ship sail on dry land." I knew I was headed in the right direction. After all, any fairies with such powerful magic must have something to teach me.

CHAPTER ELEVEN

Barry Flavored

*J*hovered over a small shop in the middle of the tall buildings that are customary in downtowns. A bright light glowed through the rooftop skylight on the small building. The music continued to play loudly as if no one else was in this part of the city. As it turned out, no one was.

I floated closer to the roof and looked down through the skylight that I'm certain didn't offer much sun light as a result of the towering office buildings surrounding the shop. Inside was a young man laying plates of food and pitchers of water on a stack of hard wood boards. Beautiful oak one-by-sixes lay atop a small stack of oak two-by-twos. There was a stack of mechanical drawings draped atop the wood. The young man danced away singing with the music until the music suddenly stopped. I next saw him crossing the floor with his jacket. All the lights except one went off.

I heard a large door slam followed shortly by a car starting and driving away. I checked my body for any pulling sensations and only noticed my strained right rudder wing.

"Well, looks like this is the place," I said to myself.

I lifted the skylight glass and fluttered into the shop. The window-like skylight slammed closed behind me. The shop was much larger inside than it appeared from the skyward angle. Around the outside edges of the large room were numerous pieces of professional woodworking equipment. There was a planer and a radial arm saw. I saw a lathe and a drill press and a band saw on another wall. In the middle of it all was a work table that also housed the all-important table saw. Everything looked as if it had never been used.

The skylight I chose to fly through was positioned in the front of the shop where the wood lay. There were two other piles, one of maple and one of birch, that I couldn't see before. All were ready to be transformed into what looked like a hutch, a desk, and a bed according to the drawings draped over the materials. Beside the sketches was the food. And when I say food I mean food with a capital "F". There were meats and cheeses and fruits of many flavors. There were vegetables and fresh breads and desserts to savor. I looked around and saw no one or no thing that could possibly eat this much food. I was hungry though and there was a strawberry that had my name on it. As I reached for the big, beautiful, red berry I heard a voice behind me say calmly.

"I wouldn't do that if I were you."

I turned and looked up into the darkness as a dark-skinned fairy with tight cornrows in his hair fluttered down into the light. He was the same size as me but was very defensive and untrusting.

"Don't even touch it. They get mad if their food is touched before they get a chance to eat it," he said.

"Who are they?" I asked.

"They are the ones who make the furniture," he replied.

"Who are you?" I asked.

"I am the fairy that lives here. Who are you?" he countered.

"I am Aynil."

"Aynil? How do you spell that?"

"A-Y-N-I-L"

"Looks like Anal"

"It's Scottish," I lied. Technically I didn't really lie because the "ay" combination of letters is often pronounce as a hard "I" in Scotland. More than anything I was too hungry to explain everything properly.

"So Aynil with a hard I sound, why are you here?"

I felt myself adapting. I needed to be confident. I began to talk with the same attitude this fairy was presenting.

"I don't know. I go where the spirit takes me," I challenged.

"What if I don't want you here?"

"Then I suggest you take it up with the higher power that sent me here. I'm sure they'll be able to help you find someplace else to go where you will be more comfortable. You do know that travelers have the right of way, don't you?"

This one line put an end to the confrontation. Most fairies know of the unwritten rule about travelers and rights of way. Because we essentially travel for an entire colony, we have priority over all other fairies except law enforcement and emergency assistants.

"How long are you going to be here?" he asked maintaining his attitude.

"Heck if I know," I replied.

"Damn!" he remarked and flew toward the rafters.

"So, what's your name?" I called up to him.

"You don't need to know my name," he replied.

"Man, you are a trip." I fluttered just above the floor in the middle of the shop. "You probably don't have a name, do you?"

"What kind of momma you think I got that wouldn't give me a name?" he yelled from the rafters.

"Did she tell you not to share it with anyone?"

"She told me not to talk to strangers."

"Well you already broke that rule didn't you?"

This guy was a real piece of work. I had never encountered anyone like this in all my travels. And he was starting to tick me off which must have been part of my adapting also because it was a new feeling for me.

"What if you get hurt and I have to call your mother? What am I supposed to say when I get her on the phone. 'Your son, whose name I don't know, is hurt?'"

"My momma's only got one son."

"Yo, it's just a name," I said.

"If it's just a name then call me whatever you want," he said.

"Whatever I want?" I inquired.

"Sure. Whatever you want," he replied.

"And you'll answer to it?" I confirmed.

"If I think it's important," he answered.

"And if you don't like it you have to tell me your real name." He did not respond. "Yo, I've got to have some way to communicate," I added. There was a moment of silence.

"Deal," he said reluctantly.

"This could be fun. Let's see," I started. "You good at anything?"

"Nothing you need to know about."

"You especially like any kind of foods?"

"I like lots of foods. I might like every kind of food as far as you know," he said.

"Alright. Alright," I said, "you want to be that way. Here we go. The first thing I seen about you was your dark skin. It's almost black."

"You ain't calling me blacky!" he protested.

"Blacky would be easy to remember but it lacks style. I gots to have style. Maybe something European. I got it. The Spanish word for black is Negro."

"No, no, no," he said. "You definitely ain't giving me no 'n' word for a name. This game is over."

"Then let's have it," I demanded.

He hesitated.

"Barry," he said.

"Barry?" I confirmed. "What's wrong with Barry?"

"Ain't nothin' wrong with Barry if you're a white guy from the midwest or a black guy in Hawaii with an African last name. Out here, brothers got names like Darnel and Prince and Marquan. Sure, once in awhile you get a Bobby or Kevin but not Barry."

"How'd your momma come up with Barry?" I asked.

"She said I was named after a football player and a singer."

"Shoot man, I was named after a Beatles song." My stomach growled. "I need to eat something."

"Sorry man, you can't eat any of that right now. You'd better get away from the food before they see you or before you get your scent on it. Come on up here. I think I got some crackers."

CHAPTER TWELVE

An Elf Problem

*H*ours passed as Barry and I sat perched on a shelf twenty feet above the untouched banquet below. I brushed cracker crumbs from my vest while admiring the strawberry I almost had. My stomach growled loud enough to startle Barry.

"Want some more crackers?" said Barry.

"No thanks."

"Don't worry," he said. "Everyone eats when the work is done."

"How long will that be?" I asked.

"Once they get here, a couple hours."

"Who are they again?"

"Them," said Barry as he pointed to a dark corner of the shop.

From between the band saw and the lathe strode a platoon of small, human-looking creatures. Each wore identical clothing and carried hand tools. Some had hammers. A couple had saws. Others had hand drills and awls. All of the tools were very old or at least rugged.

"Elves," said Barry.

"Elves? Elves aren't real. They're just creatures from human tales," I replied. The smaller elves carefully carried the multiple plates of food to the power tools and set them down. I quickly understood why the tools looked brand new.

"Really? Then what are we looking at now?" asked Barry sarcastically. This drew the attention of the largest of the elves who raised one hand above his head. The other elves froze in their tracks. He looked in our direction.

"Are you talking to me, fairy?" came a stern, powerful voice from below.

"Why do you care, Girkin?" answered Barry.

"It didn't sound like something you would say to me," replied Girkin. "Is there someone else here I should know about?"

"It's just another fairy sent to help," said Barry.

Girkin's eyes scanned the rafters for me to no avail. "Show this other fairy to me," said the frustrated elf.

Barry looked at me, "you better let him see you or no one eats tonight. Don't get too close."

I fluttered into the light and hovered close enough to the floor that they could see me but not close enough that they could touch me. My wings were still the worn burlap of the traveler. I did not have time to convert them. The elves remained frozen.

"He does not look like you," said Girkin to Barry.

"He is a traveler fairy," replied Barry.

"How do we know we can trust him?"

"You don't trust fairies anyway. Why should he be different?" countered Barry.

"That is true," said Girkin and he turned his attention to me.

"Where are you from?" he asked.

"I am from many places but I started my journey far west of here in a place called Colorado," I answered.

"I have not heard of this Colorado," he said.

"You haven't heard of Flint," remarked Barry. "Aynil here is with me. Just do your work and let us do ours and we can all eat."

Girkin stared into my face as if an answer to my trustworthiness was written in my wind-burned cheeks and the lines around my eyes. Then he reluctantly lowered his hand. The other elves continued what they had started. In minutes the food was all moved and the small shop looked like a construction zone. Planks of wood were spread out across the floor with elves measuring and marking boards to be cut. Older elves read the sketches and relayed information to the others. Saw elves, using only the tools they brought, cut more quickly and with more precision than any power tool. Boards were planed, edges were sanded, and all without a single speck of saw dust to be seen. Barry reclined on the shelf as I watched these amazing creatures work.

"This is impressive," I remarked.

"They are very good at what they do," said Barry.

"What do you do?" I asked Barry.

"'What do I do?'" Barry repeated the question as if I should know the answer. Then he did it again.

"What do I do?"

"Yeah," I said. "I see them building the stuff."

"Are you really asking me this?" he said. "I do what all fairies do; I make it special."

"You do what?!"

"I make it special."

"And how do you do that?" I inquired a bit sarcastically.

"With magic. I really shouldn't be surprised that a fairy that ain't never seen an elf doesn't know this," he proclaimed. "Let me ask you something. What kinds of jobs do your fairies back home do?"

I thought of the jobs of my parents and my friends.

"My mother is a godmother," I said.

"Nice job if someone doesn't give you a cat. What about your father?"

"He's a woodland fairy."

"What's a woodland fairy?"

"He makes the leaves green in the summer and makes them change color in the fall," I explained.

"Okay, good. So what happens when he doesn't do his job?"

"Everything looks gray."

"So would you say he makes things special?"

"Yeah, he makes things special," I said.

"If you haven't noticed, we don't got a lot of trees in the city. I work here," he answered. "Elves are good at making stuff. They make shoes, cookies, electronic devices, and furniture. They are meticulous, detailed, awesome craftsman. They can build anything from any picture you give them but they can't give it that little something that makes it special. That is what we do. Fairies have never been known for being detail oriented. Nothing we do requires us to be real precise. But what we can do is make something unique. I do that with the finish I put on the wood when the elves are done building. The functionality of the item comes from the construction. The beauty comes from the finish. Fairies provide the beauty."

"That sounds pretty arrogant," I said.

"Arrogant but true. Think it over," he said.

So I thought it over as I watched the elves below assemble the perfectly matched boards. Each piece slid or tucked or dropped effortlessly into place without even a tap of a hammer. Held together only with glue joints and dowels, each finished piece of furniture was perfect. Not a sliver of wood hung over an edge. Each corner was perfectly square. The drawers glided as if on tiny wheels closing snugly against the smoothly finished face. And nowhere was there a scrap piece of wood or a drip of glue to be found.

Girkin inspected each piece of furniture while the others stood at attention beside the pieces they had built. He gave no indication of satisfaction or displeasure as he checked the squareness of the joints and levelness of the desktops. At one point he looked one elf in the eye making him cower briefly. The shop was silent. Girkin stepped away from the hutch and brushed his hands against each other.

"We are done fairy," stated Girkin. "We will eat now."

"It's about time," said Barry under his breath. Girkin pretended not to hear him.

"Guess it's time I show you how to do this," Barry said to me. He pulled a dark, twisted stick from his shirt sleeve. "You're gonna need a wand. Any stick will do as long as it came from a tree. Can't be no plastic thing. You got a stick?"

I slid the piece of whittled cherry wood from my frontpack.

"Nice stick," said Barry. He turned his attention to Girkin. "My friend wants some strawberries," said Barry. "Make sure he gets his."

Girkin glared at Barry who floated cautiously down from his perch and surveyed the completed items. "We don't need you to make these special," said the elf leader. "Our craftsmanship is superior to anything humans can do even with their fancy tools."

"Go eat and let me do my job," said Barry.

Girkin, untrusting, glared at Barry and then at me. "Leave the traveler some strawberries," he announced to the other elves then trod toward a plate of meats and cheeses.

Wherever You Are, Be There

$\mathcal{I}$t had been two months since I arrived. Snow now laid six inches thick atop the skylight through which the light from the sky no longer penetrated. Cold pressed its way through the small human door every time it was opened and tried to completely take over the small shop when the loading bay door was raised for lumber deliveries. Every day I was thankful that I had a warm place to stay and food to eat which I earned with my newly learned skill.

I became a nocturnal creature as a result of our work and there were occasions when I was still awake in the morning when the humans picked up their new furniture. It was a delight to see the joy on their faces when they first saw their custom made tables and chairs and hutches and chests and anything else you could make out of wood. Their smiles grew wider as they opened drawers and rocked in chairs. Then they slid their hands across the rich finish and felt the magic; the magic that connected them with the item; the magic that brought them and the wood and the glue and the finish together as one. Now it was theirs. They knew that that desk or pantry or whatever it was, was made for them and no one else. They gladly handed over their money – an amount three to four times what they would pay for human-made items at a furniture store.

As it turned out, the young shop owner was a creative sort. He was not good with tools but had a knack for the art of design and everything the elves built and we finished was created and drawn by him. So, while Barry and I would like to take credit for all of the magic, we must also honor the young man who was wise enough to create the item in the first place.

The young man would spend his days working with the humans on designs, buying lumber, and shopping for food which he laid out every night. The amount of food varied by the amount of work. It was always four trays of food—one meats and cheeses, one breads and crackers, one fruits and desserts, and one of fresh vegetables—for each item built. There were nights when the elves barely had room to put all the trays of food on the pristine power tools. Nights of building three and four items were usually rare but were becoming more common as the humans' special winter holiday approached.

My wings finished their conversion within a week of arriving. They looked like beautiful knotty pine with a lacquer finish. All except for my right rudder which still looked like worn burlap and was still sore from the billboard accident. It was obvious to Barry and the elves that I still couldn't turn quickly to the right.

Girkin did not like that I was still around. He would glare at Barry and me and whisper to the other elves while he ate. It was all a bit disconcerting.

"You are a fast learner, traveler," Girkin called up to me as I slurped a juicy bite from a slice of cantaloupe. "Will you be doing my job next?"

I just smiled back.

Girkin went back to huddling with the other elves.

"Keep your eyes on them," said Barry. "And don't get too close. I see you flutterin' down around them sometimes when you are finished and I get nervous. Elves are insecure and, if you couldn't tell, they don't like us. Stay as high above them as you can at all times. You never know what they may be up to. Whatever you do, don't let them get a hold of you. Their grip is relentless."

"You worry too much," I said. "Back home we didn't worry…"

"Well you ain't home no more," he interrupted. "You're here and you need to be here, I mean all here, mind and body. Especially when you are down around those elves.

There it was, the second of the phrases from the cottonwood tree. Wherever you go, be there. It obviously wasn't said the same way but I now understood what it meant. If I was to do my job well, I needed to stay in the moment. I needed to experience what was around me.

"I worry just enough," added Barry, "just enough to not get caught and eaten by elves. Stay focused when you're down there."

With that, he fluttered up to his perch in the rafters folded his wings tightly against his back and went to sleep.

CHAPTER FOURTEEN

A Relentless Grip

The next night the young man put out twenty plates of food. It was the largest assembly of elves I had ever seen. Again they measured and sawed and joined and glued until everything was built to perfection. There was the usual desk with a hutch, plus a bed with two nightstands, a large pantry, and a chest of drawers. But tonight, amongst all the typical home furnishings, was a home. In the middle of the large items sat a three-feet-tall by two-feet-wide house. It had two floors with a roof and rooms and furniture. It looked just like some of the human houses I had seen before.

"We are done, fairies. We will eat now," called Girkin as he did every night.

"Which ones you want?" Barry asked me.

"I want the house," I grinned.

"Do the chest of drawers too. I think they go together. I'll get the rest," said Barry.

I thought I would do the chest first. I fluttered above the large object trying to absorb the energy that the future owners had sent to the sketches done by the young man. But my attention was continually drawn to the house on the floor. It became obvious that the energy I was looking for was centered in the house. I floated down to the open side and looked in. The detail was amazing. There were couches and chairs for the living room, beds and dressers for the bedrooms, and lamps and stoves and windows that opened. Each room had its own fireplace.

Visions of colors filled my head. I would paint the interior walls with a soft, semi-gloss coat using two colors on the walls. I would paint all of the window and floor trim a bright white as well as the chair rails. The floors would get a light oak stain and a clear coat finish to show off the wood. The outside would be beige with rose-colored trim and white accents.

I raised my wand above my head to begin but stopped suddenly when I felt a leathery hand grip my right leg. A sharp pain shot through my rudder wing as I tried to dart quickly to the right. I looked down to see the long fingers of one of the smaller elves wrapped around my ankle.

"I got him," shouted the elf.

Girkin spun around and ran in my direction.

Barry twisted in the air to see me tethered to the ground by the elf and Girkin heading toward me followed by other large elves.

"Fly!" yelled Barry. "Get him off you!"

Quickly, I shot high up into the rafters of the shop. Dragging the creature behind, I whipped around posts and between support beams. I shot into the air and down toward the ground making violent turns but no amount of maneuvering would shake the creature free. Down below, the other elves ran in circles, their necks craned toward the ceiling as they tried to follow our erratic flight. The aerial acrobatics continued longer than they had expected as a result of my conditioning from flying such long distances as a traveler. I could feel the skin on my leg becoming raw from the elf gripping the same spot. I was getting tired and would have to stop soon.

"I need to rest," I yelled to Barry. "What do I do?"

"Bring the boy down here," said Girkin.

"No!" yelled Barry. "They'll take you away somewhere."

"We only want our boy. If he falls from that height he will be injured. Elves are not meant to reach great heights," said Girkin. "Bring him down to us and you can finish your work."

"Don't do it Aynil. Don't trust them," warned Barry.

I was too tired to fight the grip of the elf but not ready to trust Girkin. With a last great effort, I pulled myself and my unwanted passenger up to the rafters of the shop and sat on a cross member. The little elf kept his grip on my leg as it, and he, dangled from the two-by-four twenty feet above the concrete floor.

Barry flew quickly to my new location and started yelling at the elf at the end of my leg. "Now you've done it, haven't you? Now you got yourself stuck up here in the sky with nothing to do but hold on for dear life. You should've let go when he was draggin' your little green butt across the floor."

Barry's diatribe was interrupted by the now booming voice of Girkin.

"Leave the young one alone fairy! Back away from the child or we will launch our tools with such accuracy that there will be no safe place for you in this shop."

"Throw your tools and know that at least one will hit your boy," hollered back Barry.

"You're not helping the situation," I said curtly. "Leave us alone. I can handle it from here."

"You haven't been here long enough to know these guys," said Barry.

"I know they can't reach me up here," I countered. "Leave me and the little one alone. I'll figure something out."

With that, Barry flew to a shelf high above the shop floor and waited like the elves below.

"He will not let go without my say," Girkin called out to me. "Bring him down and I will talk with him."

A fall from this height for a creature only one foot

tall would be equal to an average human falling from a ten story building. Whoever this was, he didn't deserve that fate. I looked down to the frightened little boy elf.

"Are you scared?" I asked.

"I will not say," said the elf. The eyes of his scratched face said otherwise.

"I am comfortable here where I am. I will not take you back down right now," I said to him.

The small face looked down to the ground and the other elves gathered below him then back up to me.

"If I fall, they will catch me," said the elf.

"Then they will be injured too," I said.

"That is what is expected," said the elf.

The elf looked again at the great distance between him and the floor and the smallness of those who would catch him.

"Would you prefer to sit on the beam with me and be comfortable?" I offered.

He hesitated before saying "I must hold on to you or my father will think I have given up."

"Who is your father?"

"Girkin," he said.

"I will give you my hand," I said and reached down toward him.

With his free hand, he grasped my left hand and held on tightly to both my hand and leg as if he wouldn't release either.

"Is that what you really want to do?" I asked.

After a moment of contemplation, he let go of my leg and I pulled him up to the rafters. He sat beside me, holding firmly to my left hand, while watching the commotion he had caused down below. The elves searched the building for items they could assemble into a ladder. With no scraps of wood or metal around, they set their sights on the unused power tools that surrounded the room. They were careful not to touch the items they made that night.

I looked at the scrapes on my leg from the incredible grip the elf had held. "So," I began, "what's your name?"

"I am Mitre, the fourth son of Girkin," he said.

Below us the elves labored to move the large table saw that would serve as the base of whatever pyramid they would construct to reach Mitre.

"Don't they ever give up?" I asked.

"It is not in our nature to give up. Only to continue going forward even when we know we cannot be victorious," said the elf.

"Why did you grab my leg?"

"It is what I was told to do by my father."

"Why?" I asked.

"He wanted to catch you."

"Why?" I asked again.

"Because you are a fast learner," he answered.

"Why does that bother him?"

"I think he thinks you will learn our craft and take our jobs," said Mitre. "Jobs are scarce for us now that there is automation. We can build anything but robots can build them for free."

Girkin was protecting his family. Without building furniture, the elves would have no source of food or a place to live—wherever that was.

Below us the elves had somehow gotten the lathe on top of the table saw. The base of the band saw scraped across the floor as they pushed and dragged it closer to the stacked power tools.

"I am not here to take anyone's job," I said to Mitre. "I do my share to earn my keep while I am here. I will not be here forever."

"But you have been here two full moons already. When will you be leaving?" asked Mitre.

"I don't know. I leave when I am pulled by the great fairy spirit."

"When will that be?"

"When I have learned what I came here to learn."

"What is it that you came here to learn?"

"I don't know."

"So if you will be here working until you have learned what you came here to learn," reasoned Mitre, "and you don't know what it is you are here to learn, then you could be here forever."

"It hasn't worked out that way yet," I said.

Down below the elves had leaned the tall band saw against the table. With one end of an electricity extension cord tied to the top and the other end being pulled by twenty elves on the other side of the table saw, the band saw began to scrape its way onto the table.

"They're coming to get him, Aynil!" yelled Barry.

"I am surprised they are doing so well," said Mitre. "We are not creative people. We typically work only from the plans that are given to us."

This situation could not end well if it continued on this path. I had to consider my options. I could leave the wood shop in the middle of winter, dragging a small companion with an intolerable grip only to be pulled back to face the same place and situation again because I hadn't learned what I came to learn. I could stay and hold hands with the son of the master elf until they somehow reached me and took me away to a place only elves know and that couldn't possibly be suited for fairies. Or I could start talking to Girkin and work out a compromise.

"Girkin," I yelled down to the large elf.

"What are you doing?" hollered Barry. "You can't talk to them."

"What do you want traveler?" answered Girkin.

"Is it good that you damage the human's tools?"

"We have worked for this family for five generations. He will understand," said Girkin.

"But you ruin the mystique with every scratch you

make. How does he sell his magic to the humans with scratches on his saws and lathe? With no magic, there will be no work. With no work, there will be no food," I said.

Girkin raised his large, callused hand and all the elves stopped. The shop was instantly quiet—so quiet that you could have heard the elves breathing if they had not been holding their breath waiting for their next instruction. Girkin knew he had gone too far. A defeated look came across his face as he looked toward the ground and said, "but you have my son."

"Mitre is not in danger," I said. I pushed our two hands forward to show Girkin that Mitre still held my hand. "He still holds my hand so as to not disappoint you. Mitre is very loyal and very kind and very respectful. I would feel a great pain if something bad were to happen to him. I promise you I will hold his hand as tightly as he holds mine to ensure that he is not harmed."

Girkin stared at me as he did when he was first asked to trust me. I did not look away. Girkin lowered his great hand and said calmly to the elves, "put the tools back."

With that, everything went in reverse. The band saw was being placed back on the floor. The lathe was lowered to the ground and the table saw appeared to be sliding back to its original position. In minutes they had cleared a landing area directly below us. I was just about to warm up my wings when I realized something.

"Girkin!" I called down.

Girkin again raised his large hand. Again everything stopped. "What do you want traveler?"

"I want to not be grabbed or injured when I return your son," I demanded.

"Contrary to what your friend might think, we do not eat fairies," said Girkin. "You are safe. Now, may we continue?"

I nodded my head, Girkin lowered his hand, and the elves went back to replacing the tools. The sound of metal scraping across metal and plastic wheels rolling across the concrete floor was the background music to which Mitre and I would descend.

"Hold on," I said to Mitre as I began flapping my wings. I leaned forward and pulled the small elf with me. I felt a jolt as the dead weight of Mitre pulled my arm to my side and flipped me sideways momentarily. Flapping my wings faster to adjust for the cargo, I straightened myself, squared my shoulders, took a deep breath, and began dropping slowly through the air until first Mitre, then I, touched down safely on the floor. Mitre raised our hands to show that he had maintained his grip.

"You may let go now, Mitre. You may eat," said his father. Mitre released his grip, glanced once more at me, and left to get some food and tell the other small elves of his wild ride.

Girkin turned his attention to the huge scratches on the side of the band saw that resulted from the elves' attempts to reach his son. The scratches were deep and long and he knew that what I had said about the magic was true. I stood behind him as I looked at the damage.

"Can you fix the scratches?" I asked.

"Just as we cannot take the knots out of the wood, we cannot fix the scratches."

"I can fix the scratches," I said.

"I know," said Girkin.

"How do you know?"

"I have worked with fairies before. Fairies were not here until three generations ago. Fairies came to the family through a human wedding and a child. The new family was close with fairies like you. The child did not like to follow the plans. The child did not enjoy building with boards and glue and instead was a story teller and performer and builder of dreams."

"Did the child dislike elves?" I asked.

"The child loved everything, even elves. The child would work hard in the garden to grow the food then help the father lay the food out for our families. The child would stay into the night to see the magic we would do and create great stories about each piece we built to entertain the elves while we ate."

"Where is this child now?"

"The child is old now and lies in a bed. He is

surrounded by fairies that write what his mind sees but he can no longer say. The house where you were grabbed is from the old boy's mind. It is for his great granddaughter that he will never know."

A great granddaughter he will never know? The man he spoke of was dying. The man that was once a child that told stories as the elves worked and ate was spending his last days surrounded by the fairies he had introduced to these elves. He could not speak so he created the house in his mind and the fairies drew what he imagined. They drew that which would be his legacy. A house. A house of dreams and heartbreak. A house of facts and fiction. A house of life and ultimately death. A house; or better yet, a home. For home has all of these things and that is why home is where we all long to be.

"You don't fear that I will take your job, do you?" I asked.

"I have not seen a fairy that has the constitution to do what we can."

"Then why would Mitre grab me?"

Girkin still looking at the scratch in the metal saw said, "I know that house. I know it very well."

I walked around to the front of the large elf so I could see his face. "Would you like to decorate the house?" I asked.

"We would like to help."

Girkin started by telling me the story of the house. The exterior was a replica of the house the boy had grown up in with each room an exact duplicate of a room from one of the many years of his life. Girkin had known the child for most of his life and remembered the rooms exactly as they had been decorated. It turns out that elves have even better memories than fairies. We began where every life begins—in the nursery. I tested shade after shade of light blue on the lower wall until I had the perfect color according to Girkin. The chair rail was basic white, as was the top half of the wall, which made that easier. We matched the paint on the furniture to that on the wall and the elves carved small toys to match those the boy had played with. This amount of detail continued for each room of the nine-room house. When we were finally done, Girkin and the other elves did something I had never seen them do before, they smiled. Barry could see that the effort of matching colors and textures to the memory of an elf had taken its toll on me and offered to do the finish on the dresser. He was done in about ten minutes.

There was only an hour left before the young man would be back. We all ate together, sharing stories of my travels and their history. It turns out that the distrust between Barry and the elves stemmed from their lack of familiarity. Barry was adopted into the young man's fairy family and did not know the history of this group of elves. Where he came from, elves were angry ground dwellers that would eat anything in sight—even a fairy that flew too low.

"We will eat just about anything," said Girkin. "But not you. We know we need you as much as you need us. It is from both of our efforts that the greatest magic comes."

The elves gathered the empty food trays and swept away all specks of dirt and any crumb that might have landed on the floor. The power tools were placed back where they belong. Barry and I used our wood and metal finishing talents to repair the scratches. Everything looked newer than ever. Then I felt a short tug on my vest. I looked down to see Mitre holding a tray toward me with a single strawberry.

"You will be leaving soon, won't you?" he asked.

"I don't know," I said.

"You will be leaving soon," Mitre said confidently.

"It is time," called Girkin as the first glow of morning crept into the corner of the window. The elves began methodically filing out of the shop.

"The world looks very different from up high," said Mitre as a grin appeared on his little face. "I hope I will get to see it from there again."

I took the tray with the strawberry as he turned to join the others. Mitre's eyes and mouth returned to their standard, stoic appearance as he marched quickly toward his father who was careful to check each elf as they passed. Mitre was the last of the small army to scurry into the dark corner from which the elves had come every night. I held the strawberry in one hand while I turned to place the empty tray among the others atop the table saw.

"Is that is a good strawberry?" asked Girkin.

I looked down at my small reward for the work we had done that eventful night. "It's the best I've ever had," I answered.

"Then, I am happy," said Girkin and he turned and trod into the darkness.

The clicking sounds of the door locks echoed in the empty building as the young man opened the doors to a new world that had changed overnight. He must have known something was different because today he walked slower and, with his eyes closed, he dragged his hand over each piece of furniture as if it held a memory he didn't want to forget. But it was the house that made him stop walking and sit down on the floor beside it. A gentle finger rocked the rocking chair. He moved the furniture and played with the miniature toys in the nursery. A tear trickled down his cheek as he sat in the middle of the vacant shop.

"Thank you," he said aloud.

That was all it took to start that tingling feeling in my leg. Mitre was right. I was being pulled.

CHAPTER FIFTEEN

Boys With No Father, Mother or Sister

*N*ever fly in the rain.

Commandment number one and the first thing they teach you in flight school. Fairy wings are not as waterproof as, say, bird wings. Our wings are more like those of a butterfly, or a bee if you are a tooth fairy or mischief fairy. I was zooming over some place with hills and trees when the sky opened up and, what seemed like water balloons, started pelting me. "My wings are soaking up water faster than a sponge at a car wash," I said out loud. Then I wondered "where did that come from?"

I wasn't so much thinking about the idea of taking on water as much as I was wondering why I used a metaphor to describe it. I was blending and I was in The South. And with each blob of water that my wings absorbed, I got closer and closer to The South. I was going down and if I didn't find a place to land soon, I was going down hard.

In the distance I saw the glow of candlelight from a small cabin. I beat my wings one great time to shake loose whatever water I could and glided down toward the beacon. I lit on the ground under a tree and caught my breath. The air tasted like mint and pine and lilacs. I know it sounds funny to say that air tasted like anything but it was so thick from the rain and I was breathing through my mouth. The heavy rain drops pounding on the thick cover of sassafras leaves reminded me why I had dropped in. My wings too wet for any subtle flying, I stumbled toward the glow in the distance.

Now within one hundred yards of the cabin, I made sure my bulletproof frontpack was secure. As I neared the cabin, I heard the sound of a harmonica playing a dark tune.

"Can't ya' play sumpin' more happy? It's already rainin' outside. We don't need it rainin' inside, too," said a young voice from inside the cabin.

"I don't feel like it," came the equally young-sounding reply.

"Then just put the thing away," said a third youthful voice. "I'd rather listen to the rain on the roof anyway."

And then there was silence. Not the most perfect environment for meeting people. But it was the situation I was in and apparently the place I belonged because I no longer felt an ache in my legs. I stood outside the front door listening to the sounds of raindrops hitting the roof. Then, without notice, the door gradually swung open.

Standing inside were three ragged-looking boy fairies with the same distrusting expression on their faces. One of the boys in the back had brown hair, the other had the more common red hair and the boy in the front had the rarest of hair: green. They couldn't have been more than eleven or twelve years old. I was, at first, nervous to be confronted with three angry fairy boys but quickly realized how lucky I was that they weren't humans with guns.

"Hello. My name is Aynil," I offered.

"What are you?" the green-haired boy asked.

"Are you a fairy?" asked the red-haired boy in the back.

"He's not a fairy," said the brown.

"He has wings," argued the red.

"I've never seen wings like those," said the green.

"I think he's a fairy," said the red.

"Shhhh," interrupted the green. "Are you a fairy?" he asked me again.

"I am a traveler fairy," I said.

"What's a traveler fairy?" asked the brown.

"Yeah, what's a traveler fairy?" repeated the red.

"I travel from place to place having experiences

then go back and share the stories with my colony," I explained.

"What are you doing here?" asked the green.

"My wings were wet from the rain. I'm looking for a place to dry off. Can I talk to your parents?"

"We ain't got no parents here," said the brown.

"Shhh," scolded the green.

"Why? You heard him. He's a fairy," said the brown.

"Yeah. He's a fairy," agreed the red.

"He's an adult. He might be here to take our stuff," argued the green.

"He is an adult," agreed the red.

"What do we have worth takin' anyway?" asked the brown.

"We really don't have much stuff," agreed the red.

"Our food. Our music. The other things," said the green.

"What other things?" asked the brown and red together.

"The other things. The human things," said the green slowly.

"Ohhh. The *other* things," said the red.

"What does he care about that stuff?" said the brown. "We don't even know how to use most of it. He can have it all for all I care." The brown turned his attention to me. "You said you travel places and tell stories?"

"Yes," I said.

"Have you been a lot of places?" the brown asked. By now I had been traveling for fifteen years and had hundreds of stories to tell.

"Yep," I said.

"Can you tell those stories to us?" he asked.

"Will you let me come in?" I asked.

The brown pushed the other boys away from the door and opened it wide.

"I could use a good story tonight," said the brown.

The cabin was small with three cots hanging like bunk beds one above the other. To the right were three soft perches and a table. In the middle was a small dining table with clean bowls stacked nine high in the middle and nine clean spoons beside them. The back wall had shelves filled with boxes of sugar coated cereals that you would assume young boys would prefer, and one lonely box of raisin bran. Boxes of Pop Tarts of all flavors were spread across the shelf below the cereal.

"Is that all y'all eat?" I asked.

"We were told that anything bad for humans was probably good for us," said the red.

"I think they meant berries and nuts and plants," I commented.

"They taste good," grunted the green.

"Don't you take that attitude with the traveler, Aspen," said the brown

"Now you done it! Now he knows my name,"

complained Aspen as he pushed the brown into the wall. I hoped this might lead to getting the other two names. It did.

"Who cares. I'll tell him mine if it makes you happy." The brown turned to me. "My name is Maple and him over there is Autumn."

"I can tell him my own name," proclaimed Autumn, the boy with the red hair.

"Jiminy Christmas, you gonna argue about everything, too?" said Maple to Autumn.

"Well you don't have to tell him everything yourself," argued Autumn.

"You got no right telling strangers our names," added Aspen.

"You just gonna leave him out there in the rain?" charged Maple.

"No," defended Autumn.

"No," grunted Aspen.

"If he's comin' in he might as well know our names," concluded Maple.

Aspen and Autumn stood in a silent huff and searched their minds for a rebuttal. There was none. That loss of words brought the uncomfortable silence. The uncomfortable silence that comes when no one will admit they were wrong. The silence that is like a game of chicken where the first person to talk is the loser. This one looked like it could go on for days.

Since I was the only adult in the room, I thought I should act like one.

"Aspen. Is it because of your green hair?" I asked, trying to make conversation. The green-haired boy just stared back at me. "Autumn—for the changing of the leaves?" I asked. Autumn nodded with a grin.

"Maple?" I asked in the direction of the brown-haired boy.

"It sounded better than Oak," said Aspen.

"It is nice to meet you all," I said.

I continued my stroll through the cabin. In the back corner I finally came across the "human stuff" Aspen had thought so important to conceal. There, on a table the size of their dining table was a stack of assorted items you might find in a human home. Most of the items were chrome or stainless steel but there was the occasional plastic serving spoon or item with no real explanation like a stapler.

"They're shiny," said Autumn.

Away from the other things, beside a stool on the floor, lay a rectangular, chrome-plated, hand-held device with a screen that would light up every now and then and display words. Aspen rushed to retrieve it when he noticed me looking in its direction. He put the item in his shirt pocket.

The rain pelted the roof harder.

"Sounds like we might be here awhile," said Maple.

"How's about you tell us one of your stories?"

"How's about I tell you one and you tell me one?" I bargained. After all, I was here to learn something too. "Deal?" I asked.

"Deal," said Maple.

"Deal," said Autumn.

We all waited for what would most likely be reluctance from Aspen.

"What if we don't have any stories?" asked Aspen.

"Everyone has at least one good story," I said.

"I don't," replied Aspen.

"How about you go last then? Maybe one of our stories will jog your memory," I said.

Aspen took up a perch, pulled the shiny rectangle from his pocket, and finally nodded in agreement.

The deal confirmed, I began by telling them the story of my graduation. How I had flown through the old cottonwood tree, how beautiful Flaylen was with her fairy godmother wings and finally about the banquet and send-off I received from my colony. I added how much I missed everyone and hoped to be pulled back soon. My first story completed, I turned the floor over to Maple.

CHAPTER SIXTEEN

Death's Little Helpers

*M*aple was giddy. He had never heard a story of a graduation or of traveler fairies and wanted to meet Flaylen himself. Everyone wants to meet Flaylen. The excitement settled as he realized it was time for him to reciprocate. With some trepidation, Maple began his story.

"As we said, we have no parents. We also have no brothers or sisters."

"Stop with this silly story already," interrupted Aspen. "He doesn't want to hear some sob story about some kids in a cabin in the woods."

"It's my story and I want to tell it," replied Maple.

"Just let him tell the story," said Autumn.

"You are not brothers?" I asked.

Autumn and Aspen both shook their heads 'no'. Maple continued.

"When each of us was ten years old, we were rescued from a dire situation. I was pulled from a coal

95

mine before it collapsed. No one from my colony made it out. Autumn was saved from a forest fire that took his colony. And Aspen…" Maple looked to Aspen for his permission. Aspen nodded his head. "Aspen was saved from a flood caused by a rain storm like the one outside.

"As it turns out, all three of us kind of had the same experience. A large fairy—sometimes I even think she was an angel—in dark clothes swept us up and wrapped a dark cloak around us to protect us we think. All's I remember is a calm and soothing voice saying 'shhh. You will be alright. You will be alright. This is your destiny.' It was Death," he said uneasily. "Not the Death everyone thinks about, but the softer, gentler Death. She brought each of us here and came every night to teach us. We would always have to stand on the porch and look into the darkness of the woods to hear her messages. She said we had each been chosen to be here. That we had a unique ability to do what we would be asked to do. And that we would not be allowed to return to a colony, any colony, ever again or everyone in that colony would die."

I was awe-struck. What do you say to three orphans who will never know anyone other than each other for the remainder of their lives? I said the one word I found myself saying more than any other on my journeys.

"Why?" I asked.

"Why what?" Maple returned.

There were so many "whys" that I didn't know where to start. So I just blurted them all out as they came to me.

"Why did you live while the rest of your colony died? Why did this angel rescue you? Why are there three of you? Why can't you go to another colony without everyone dying?"

Autumn and Aspen looked at Maple.

"It's your story," said Autumn wryly.

Maple addressed my questions with the one word I heard more on my journeys than any other. "Because," he started. "Because we have the ability to filter out toxins before they reach our vital organs helping us survive the most dreadful of environments. Because we were the chosen ones to do our jobs. Because the great ones did not want us to be lonely. And because we are Death's helpers and Death needs us more than any colony would."

"Death's helpers?" I asked.

The three nodded their heads solemnly. They waited patiently while I attempted to process the information.

"You said entire colonies would perish if you lived among them," I recounted. They all nodded confirmation. "Am I going to die?"

"We don't know," Maple calmly replied. "You found us. We usually go to the people and fairies we help."

The room was quiet except for the sound of the rain hammering the roof. Aspen looked up to the source of the noise and said, "We won't be helping anyone tonight."

"We will be missed tonight," said Autumn.

"Helping anyone?" I wondered aloud. "How do you help them? Who are these people you help?"

"Do you always ask more than one question at a time?" countered Aspen.

"I do, when there is more than one question to be asked," I replied rather curtly.

"There are many people and fairies who will die alone. Those are the ones we help," said Maple. "We're there for them to talk to. We help calm their fears. We give them someone to pass along the stuff they need to share. We stay with them until Death finally comes to take them to wherever they are to go next."

"Where is that?" I asked.

"We don't know," said Autumn. "Life is just an experience. You are born, you learn, and you move on."

Life sounded eerily similar to what I had done for the past fifteen years. I would pop into some place, have an experience, and leave not knowing where I was headed next. But did I learn anything? Abe said I was given experiences that would teach me something either I or the colony needed to learn. In Iowa I learned 'wherever you go, there you are' which meant to make the best of every situation and that everything happens for a reason. In Detroit I learned 'wherever you are, be there' which I took to mean that everyone must live in the moment and not worry about the future or dwell on the past. I guess I had learned a lot on my travels. What would I learn here?

"I think it's time for another story from you," said Autumn.

Though I had many more questions, I felt he was right and began the story of how I met Garland, the Traveler.

CHAPTER SEVENTEEN

Autumn and
The Lonely Old Man

The night got darker and the rain drops softened a bit. We could now hear the plopping sounds of water drops falling into the puddles that had formed around the cabin. I finished the story of Garland to the delight of the three boys who never seemed to get sleepy. Maybe their eating a box of Pop Tarts each while I spoke had something to do with it.

Aspen continued to fondle the shiny rectangular object. Occasionally he would drag his fingertip across a round area or press a button and a light would shine in the screen at the top. He would stare at the screen until it faded to dark which happened a few seconds later unless he touched the round area again or pushed another button.

"Have you seen him again?" asked Maple about Garland.

"No. But I've heard stories from others about Garland's adventures. I think he will be one of the greatest travelers this world has ever known when he's done."

"I've seen a fire like that," said Autumn, "like the one in Iowa."

"Do you want to tell me that story?" I asked.

"No," was the casual reply. "I know why it happened. I've moved on. As Death says, 'whenever you leave, go.' You can't live your life worryin' about the past. But there's a story I can tell you; a story that's important to me."

It didn't dawn on me until later that this was the third of the Great Cottonwood's four phrases from my graduation. It had been so long since I had heard one of them and this experience was so contrary to what my mission was supposed to be. But dwelling on the past is not the same as remembering the past. I was just supposed to remember. Remember and learn. Autumn's statement needed no additional explanation so I settled in to listen to his story.

"I was in trainin' and Death took me to a large hospital in the city where an old man laid in a bed all alone in a private room. There weren't no flowers. There weren't no cards wishing him well. It didn't matter 'cause he couldn't smell a flower or read a card anymore. And he couldn't talk with his mouth but he could see when he opened his eyes and he could hear. Hearin' is the last sense to go in humans.

"The room felt sterile and cold. I hovered in a corner with Death beside me as she told me of this man who would die alone. She told me that he was a great man who made a great sacrifice for the good of the world. She said that, before he came to this world, he was given a choice of two lives. The first life would bring him great wealth without no worries. It would give him a lovin' and carin' family. And, though there would be some trouble now and then, his life would be filled with happiness.

"The second life would be painful and hard and would test his constitution every day. He would become driven and determined but would never seem to get ahead. And all of this would be really hard for his family that he loved with a great heart but could not show it. While the first choice would be nice and peaceful, it was the second life that would create the children and grandchildren that would change the world. He chose the second option and, as a result, laid there alone in a hospital bed preparing to move on. He was my assignment and I stayed with him.

"Days passed and his children started to come. Each one came alone, not even bringin' pictures of their families; the families the man sacrificed for so they could change the world. But he didn't need pictures 'cause he could see them in his mind. And I could see them in his mind when he shared them with me. As I listened to the obligatory speeches given by the now grown up children, I realized that they did not know about his sacrifice.

"The oldest child came first. She was a doctor who's patience with her patients was the key to her practice. The old man said he was pretty tough on her. She was the best in her class and had a choice of any type of doctorin' she wanted but chose a small family practice–the emphasis being on family. Her and her husband had been married twenty years and she has four kids who have done some big things with art and science and there's one who wants to be a congressman.

"The youngest child came next. She is single and a lawyer who helps poor people. She will show the world how to better work together as will her daughter when that time comes.

"The middle child came, reluctantly. He was a teacher who married a teacher so they could spend the summers with their kids and not work all the time like his dad. And his kids would be writers and philanthropists and people who make the world more beautiful.

"The old man wasn't gonna be here to see those kids or how they would change the world; same as they weren't gonna ever know the sacrifice he made that moment that he chose the second option.

"So I sat all night and watched the shallow breaths of the 'skin-and-bones' remains of the old man. Eager to help any way I could, I jumped at any noise or movement. Most times it was for nothin' but I was ready. And that made me happy.

"It was another seven days before he pushed out the last of the air from his lungs and did not try to take more in. In those seven days I waited for the time when he would share some great insight or revelation about the meaning of life or why we do what we do. After seven days I realized that sometimes those moments never come. Sometimes we are left to find those answers for ourselves. Sometimes people just die, and that dying has to be okay too.

"You know, we all make sacrifices. We all have a reason for being here and we all give up somethin' somewhere. When I think of what the old man did... let's just say I felt a lot better about my situation."

CHAPTER EIGHTEEN

Aspen's Shiny Box

*A*spen was unfazed by Autumn's story. He just stared at the shiny box. I dared to ask to see it. "I learned quite a bit from the elves about how things go together," I offered. "It looks as if it might plug into something or have something plug into it."

"I know," said Aspen. "I've seen it bein' used." He dragged his finger around the dial and the screen and, after a brief moment of introspection, pushed the hand holding the box toward me.

"I'll be careful," I said as I gingerly grasped the smooth, metal object.

I rotated the box in my hands and was amazed at the simplicity. I touched the circular pad and pressed the single button until the back light of the screen glowed revealing the words "Everybody Hurts."

"There's a wire with things that go in your ears on the table that plug into that hole in the top," said Aspen.

"You want to try 'em? I'll get 'em for ya'," said Autumn as he rose.

"In my ears?" I replied. "Seems like that would be pretty distracting. Besides, it's probably not a good idea to stick human things in my ears; at least not without medical attention nearby." Autumn and Maple chuckled a little at the comment that Aspen appeared to not hear.

"I'll tell my story now, if that's alright with y'all?" Aspen said. I didn't expect to hear from the reluctant fairy that night. I settled into my perch with the shiny box in my hands and waited.

"It was winter," he began. "It was one of those cold-with-no-snow kinda winters. Those are the worst kinda winters if you ask me. Everything is brown, the sun goes down early and comes up late, and the sky threatens to snow every day but just makes everything gray instead. No one goes outside. And no one is very happy.

"The box belonged to a boy. He was almost a man but humans call most teenagers boys. Death took me to his house. She pointed at some pictures of him with his friends and his family. He had a great smile when he wasn't being too cool to use it. I expected to see someone with a grave disease or something. I thought I'd see him stuck in a bed about to pass like the old man Autumn told you about. When Death took me to his room, there was no one there.

"The room was very neat. You know, clean. The bed was made, the clothes were all put away, and the shoes were

106

lined up inside the closet. There were more pictures of the boy by himself, another of what must have been a girl-friend and one that may have been a very good friend that was a boy. There were trophies and a poster of some cheer-leaders but there was no gravely ill boy. Then we heard the sound of a door opening on the lower floor and footsteps trudging up the stairs. A little bit later the door opened and the boy walked into the room.

"He didn't look like the boy in the pictures. His hair was that fake black color, his shoulders were slumped over and he did not smile. He looked worried. He looked sad. He looked confused. He looked uncomfortable in his own room. He wore those things in his ears and held the box in his hand. He tossed his backpack on the bed and left."

"Watch him carefully for me," Death said to me. "I will be back."

"I was confused but stayed behind as she asked. I had been with many dying people but the boy looked physically fine to me.

"After awhile the boy came back into the room with two small pictures and a felt bag with something heavy in it. He still had those things in his ears. The box was in his pocket. Tears trickled down his face as he wrote "I'm sorry" on the back of the two pictures and took them out of the room. He came back in and sat on the bed beside the felt bag. He opened it very methodically and pulled out a gun.

"I tried to listen to his thoughts but only heard the music from the things in his ears and the box. I heard the words "everybody hurts" and "hold on" but could not hear his thoughts or why he needed to hear these words. I tried to talk to him but he could not hear me over the music. More "everybody hurts" and more "hold on" but the words weren't working. Why weren't they working? Then Death appeared again beside me and said 'you may go now.'"

"I can't leave!" I yelled. "We have to stop him!"

"It is not our place to stop them. We are here to make them comfortable."

"But he's not comfortable. He's sad. He's confused. He doesn't want to do this. He can't want this. Even the music is telling him to hold on. He's only a boy."

"We are here to make him comfortable," she repeated only this time her voice cracked. That was when I noticed the tears in Death's eyes. She never cried. Normally Death treated passing on as just part of the life cycle but somehow this was different. She didn't want to be there. She didn't want to take this young spirit.

"I tried again to speak to the boy but again the music blocked my words. Then there was a loud blast and he was gone – his confused spirit wrapped in Death's soothing cloak, flying away to the place known only to her and those who have gone before him; the place where we all go eventually.

"I stayed behind looking at the remains of what was a beautiful child and could only think of not being able to connect. I blamed the box and the things in the ears that kept me from reaching him. I needed to stop this from happening again, so I took it. I took his music box."

There was a moment of silence. We just sat there and listened as the wind rustled the leaves making the few water drops that still clung to them fall to the ground.

"She came back that night," said Maple, briefly looking to Aspen as if for approval. "Death, she came to us that night to help us better understand what had happened. She said 'No one comes here to die at their own hand. Those who fight through the most difficult experiences – the ones that bring you to your knees and make you say 'this is too hard' – are the ones best suited to help others in the future.'"

"She said 'it is a rare person who can empathize with others when they have not experienced great loss or heartache,'" added Amber. "'It is through the greatest losses and deepest pain that we learn the most important lessons. And those who are given the gift of these most difficult lessons, have a much greater destiny than the pain they are feeling at that moment.'"

"I asked her why she was crying," interrupted Aspen. "She said 'because taking your own life solves nothing. While his spirit is in a more peaceful place, it remains troubled and confused and still searches for the answers to the questions he ran away from.' Then I asked her 'why me? Why did you take me to his room?' She answered with the same cracking voice I heard in the bedroom, 'because I knew you would try to stop him.'

"It is a permanent solution to a temporary problem," recited Aspen. "All things must pass; this too will pass. Nothing lasts forever." Then he sighed and raised his head. "That's what I would have said to him. But he couldn't hear me."

He pushed off from his perch and fluttered in my direction. He stopped and hovered in front of me and looked into my eyes with a peacefulness uncommon to such a young face. Then he smiled and held out his hand and said, "This is not a good time to be distracted."

I smiled an understanding smile and placed the shiny box in his hand.

Through the silence came a sweet sounding breeze. It wasn't really a breeze but it sounded like a soft wind that was coated with honey. I guess it was more soothing than sweet. Whatever it was, it was familiar. It was what the boys heard every night before fulfilling their duties. The three small fairies looked at each other and rose.

"She's comin'," said Maple. "She must be mad at us."

"We couldn't leave. It was rainin'," said Autumn.

"Maybe she's not comin' for us," said Aspen.

They all looked at me. I was about to face Death.

CHAPTER NINETEEN

Facing Death

The pleasing tone continued as we swung the front door open to the lush green forest and clear night sky. The air tasted like clean dirt. The song came from a shadowy area in the woods directly out the door. I could barely make out a flowing black figure in the darkness that hovered slightly above the ground. The darkness made everything simple. There was no contrast. Everything blended into the same dark space and the dark space blended into everything. And then the music stopped and the dark cloak of Death floated forward out of the darkness. It was swift but not rushed. She stopped in front of the boys first. I could not hear what she said to them but assumed she was talking to them because they would occasionally nod in agreement. At one point I became nervous when Autumn looked in my direction and nodded again to something she said.

When she finished talking to the boys, the figure floated in my direction and stopped directly in front of me. She had no wings or legs yet the cloak did not touch the ground. Her arms raised slowly. Two pale hands lifted up from the long cloak sleeves. The long fingers of each hand gently grasped the edges of her hood and peeled it back revealing a face of simple and pure beauty.

"You are Aynil," she said. Her voice was like a warm bath. It enveloped me and caressed my skin and let me know that everything would be okay. It was obvious why someone might look forward to the time when she would take them.

"You have traveled a great distance. You have learned much more than most travelers. And you have come here - where only two other travelers have come before and have left without me taking them. I thank you for sharing your stories with the boys on this stormy night."

"Are you here to take me?" I asked.

"Do you want me to take you?" she asked.

I wondered. To some it might seem weird that I would even consider the option of passing on. But put yourself in my shoes. For fifteen years I traveled. I had gone to hundreds of places with thousands of stories and all of it alone. When I tried to stay longer in a place that felt comfortable, the pain of dragging became unbearable and I would be forced to go on-the-wing. I was tired. When would it end? I thought again of Carlin and his fifty years. How much longer would I be sentenced to go who-knows-where and to learn who-knows-what? Why would I want to do that anymore? I no longer cared if the colony needed the lessons I had learned. It was peaceful here. I'm sure it would be even better where she was going. I searched my brain for something that would make me want to stay. I thought of the boys behind me who might like some guidance. I thought of Garland and wondered where he might be. I thought about home and Barden and Joylyn and I removed my mother's hair pin from my breast pocket. The diamonds still sparkled even in this place of very little light. As I looked at it I envisioned it in my mother's hair as she went off to grant a child's wish. I saw her making breakfast with Barden on a weekend morning while I bounced around in the trees. And I remembered what she said when she gave it to me, knowing that she might not see me again. This was not a pin for holding back hair but a special gift for holding memories. I was to give it to someone with whom I would create more special memories. Flaylen.

"Do you want me to take you?" Death asked again even more gently.

"No," I said.

Death smiled.

"That is why you were allowed to come here. Take what you have learned and share it with whomever you meet," she spoke. "It is an important message that few will learn until they learn it for themselves. My boys can only do so much."

I felt the familiar tingle in my leg. It was pulling to the northwest. The smile on her face implied that she knew I was being pulled.

"How much longer will I travel?" I asked.

"Not much longer."

"Do you know where I am going now?"

She leaned into me and whispered, "You are going home."

CHAPTER TWENTY

Time Waits for No One

I did not feel the tingle in my leg that had directed me to my destinations for the past fifteen years. I didn't need it. I knew how to get home.

It was nighttime and below me the headlights of the cross-country semi-trucks shone brightly on the highway. Occasionally one would blink their peripherals to thank another for letting them know when it was safe to move over after they passed. There was no rain or bugs or branches to slow my flight, or at least I couldn't feel any. Everything passed by in a blur. I thought it was because I was flying so fast but soon realized it was because I was tired. After a night of no sleep and a full day of flying, I found myself counting the cars and trucks that dotted the freeway at this late hour to help me stay awake. I intended to get home tonight. But intentions aren't always enough and I found myself dozing off. I needed to stop and rest if just for a little while.

With only a half moon to light my way, I steered off my aerial path and into a cluster of trees beside a river. I dropped down as lightly as a fatigued fairy can and landed hard in a clearing. It felt unusually comfortable. So comfortable that I didn't bother to hide myself in the trees or bushes but instead just lay down where I had landed and immediately fell asleep.

While I slept I dreamed. I dreamed of food I hadn't eaten in fifteen years, like mountain trout and columbine nectar. I dreamed of telling stories that my colony had never heard before, like how I was there when Garland became a traveler and the special job of three orphans. And I dreamed of a home in the cotton-woods, my home, with a great big room for telling stories, and a big kitchen where I could cook all the foods I had tried, and a room with a big feather bed that wraps around you like a hug when you sleep. And with a little boy that looks like me and a little girl who looks like Flaylen. And I slept longer than usual. I think I just didn't want to wake up.

The sounds of water gently washing over rocks and radial car tires humming across asphalt are not two sounds that you would necessarily hear together unless you were near a freeway bridge that crossed a river. And given that rare combination, I doubt you would call those sounds familiar. But after a long nap, I woke up to these familiar washing and humming sounds.

A dense, early-morning fog hugged the ground and hung over the trees. As I rose I could see the glow of the fog lamps of cars and trucks as they crossed the bridge. I knew this bridge. I knew this clearing. I knew this fog. I was in Iowa.

The clearing was much more overgrown than when Garland and I shepherded forty-nine school kids to safety. I wandered around the clearing remembering where Garland stood when his voice boomed over the group and they lined up to be counted. I stood on the bank where I had seen a fiery red sun set behind a charred field. It is still the most sad and beautiful sunset I have ever seen. And I again felt the moment when Trunk and Darla said good-bye forever to their only son. And I missed them.

Hidden by the fog, I powered myself up above the thick foliage and headed toward the line of trees that once housed a colony. The road, of which my last memory is of a truck skidding to a dusty stop, was now paved with asphalt. New trees had sprung up around the charred remains of those too proud to fall after the fire. The largest of them all, the one that was our home, still reached highest into the sky. Black from trunk to top, it should have served as a reminder to all humans of the colony that was home to more traveler fairies than any other; where stories of countless different worlds and people and eras had been told; where the lessons of

117

hundreds of individual experiences were shared. But I doubt that the humans even knew we were here.

The field behind the trees was green with wavy corn stalk leafs not quite knee high to a human. It must be the month of June. The house in the distance was larger and nicer than the one I remember from the day of the fire. I did not bother to look for the house on that day. Perhaps the red fire trucks were unable to save it after all.

Everything was as I had remembered with the exception of the new house and paved road and new bushes and trees. But I guess things do that. I guess things keep growing even though you aren't there.

"Things keep growing even though you aren't there." I said it out loud. And, for the first time, I was scared of going home.

The sun rose and began burning off the fog that hid me from human view while I wasted time fluttering back and forth contemplating the many things that may have changed in my colony while I was gone. I started with the chance that my parents may have passed on. While that would definitely make me sad, it would not have been a great surprise and, besides, I think I would have somehow known if that had happened. Next was that the colony could have burned down. But our colony is in a cropping of trees in a suburb of the big city and the red fire trucks would not let a fire go so close to the human's homes. I thought of some of my friends getting injured in a leaf painting accident or something. But nothing really bothered me until I thought of the two little kids I had seen in my dream and considered that they were not mine. That Flaylen had married someone else. This thought didn't just bother me, it physically hurt me. It hurt my head when I thought of it. It made my wings too weak to fly and my knees too weak to stand. It made my heart stop for moments that felt like hours. It was the only thing I feared.

But I would have known it, wouldn't I? She and I are too close for me to have not felt something. It probably would have felt a lot like I'm feeling now but at least I would have known. "This isn't fair," I yelled to the hum of tires on the highway.

"So what do I do if this has actually happened?" I rationalized. "Rebecca is pretty and smart and athletic. But she's got that mother issue thing going on plus she's a huge flirt. What am I worried about? There are a bunch of tammies in the colony. I'm a traveler. I can get any girl I want. I don't need Flaylen. Heck, I don't even know what she looks like. So what if she got married and had twelve kids and they all look like her and...and..."

And it wasn't helping. My wings still hurt. My knees still felt weak. Then I heard a clank sound and felt a dull thud in my chest. A half-second later came the sound of a gun being fired. I ran my fingers across my front pack and felt the tear and the dent left by what must have been a bullet. I heard the sound of something whizzing past followed by another gun shot. I looked toward the highway and saw a pick-up truck parked on the shoulder and a human taking aim for another shot. There's nothing like a life-or-death situation to get you to quit moping and take action. I was going home whether Flaylen wanted me or not.

CHAPTER TWENTY-ONE

Always Remember
Your Name

June in Colorado is the best time of year. Of course June in every place in North America seems to be the best time of year. Everything is green, the days are long, the temperatures are perfect, and the bugs are few and small. I took my time flying the last few kilometers of my trip. I wanted to admire the places I had not seen for so long. I wanted to see what had changed over the past fifteen years. Most of all, I wanted to delay the pain of seeing Flaylen holding a child that wasn't mine.

Over the last hundreds of kilometers I had made some decisions. One was that I would call Barden and Joylyn, "Dad" and "Mom". I had come to realize that, in most cases, the words were not simply labels but, even when said in anger, were filled with love and respect. I decided that I would not waste too much time before endeavoring into a new field. Woodland fairy doesn't seem so bad if I can do things to protect the trees. But the most important of my decisions was how to handle the Flaylen dilemma. To find the answer, I reflected on each of my experiences over the past fifteen years. I recounted the people and situations and lessons. And while each place had its own unique \lesson, the one underlying message was the last thing the cottonwood tree had told me: always remember your name. Aynil. A name given to me by two people that saw more in me on the day I was born than I may ever believe to be true. A name that, when spoken, elicits curious expressions from those around. A name that, when explained, held the answer to every problem I encountered. Aynil—an acronym for All You Need Is Love. While I may not like that the girl I had longed for all my life could be with someone else, there was no way I could not love her. I removed my mom's hairpin from my breast pocket intent on giving it to Flaylen when next I saw her.

With that decided, I turned in the direction of the place I had not seen in fifteen years. I heard music playing in the distance and remembered the day I had started my journey to who-knows-where and for who-knows-how-long. I wondered who the new traveler was and hoped only the best for him or her. I can now see why they send the new ones off before the old one returns. If I had talked to Tappin, I doubt I would have ever left. The music got louder and a faint glow showed in the trees up ahead. I turned to watch the sun dip behind the foothills. I would be lying if I said I remembered every sunset I ever saw but I knew I would remember this one. It would be my last sunset as a traveler.

While the sun sank, so did I. The fatigue of years of flying was catching up to me. It's a tired you only feel when you know all of your work is done—that you are not putting something off until tomorrow. A tired that says your mind, as well as your body, can rest. It was a tired that wanted only a soft featherbed to lay in that would wrap around you like a hug. When the sun was about to disappear into the shadow of a mountain, I heard a soft, pleasing, familiar voice say, "welcome home stranger."

The soft light of dusk illuminated the face I had longed to see. It was Flaylen. "I hope you plan on staying," she said.

"I will need a very good reason," I answered.

She wrapped her arms around my neck, pulled her body against me, and gently pressed her lips to mine. It was a gentle but firm kiss that seemed to breathe life back into my ragged body. I think it would have brought me back from the dead if needed. She pulled herself away and grasped my hand with a firmness not felt since Mitre grabbed my leg.

"Let's go home and get those wings off," she said.

CHAPTER TWENTY-TWO

Home

*B*arden and Joylyn were waiting just outside the clearing. They looked the same as the day I left. Joylyn could see the sparkle of her hair pin in Flaylen's hair as she and I approached hand in hand. My mother and father bowed briefly to the two of us before wrapping their arms around my neck and pulling in tightly. I guess they missed me, too.

The party lasted for five days—I couldn't hold my wings on any longer. What I was never told about coming home was how the rest of the colony actually wanted the returning traveler to keep their wings as long as possible. The party would continue until the traveler dropped his wings. This meant no work or school until the traveler committed to staying. I was encouraged to keep going to break the record of the other travelers. It turns out the old record was only two days and not seven like the more jubilant fairies kept telling me so they could keep partying. Flaylen refused to let go of my hand the entire time.

Flaylen and I were married soon after my return. We have a nice home with a large living room for telling stories and a big kitchen for cooking exotic food. And we have two children; a little boy who looks like me and a little girl who looks like her. They call us 'Mom' and 'Dad'. Grandpa Barden reads them a few pages of his novel whenever he gets a chance.

I took some time off to consider what I might do for my next job. It had to be something that kept me available to others since I am still the resident Traveler and still have stories to share. I chose to be a tooth fairy. I'm still not excited about trading money for something that comes out of a human's mouth but, after the years of experiences I had, it was hard to give up the thrill of the chase and the unknown. I also must admit, there are times when I'm out on a tooth route that I get the feeling of being pulled. The feeling now comes from a small part of my heart and not my leg. Tooth fairy wings are built for short sprints and would not withstand the rigors of long-distance flying. So, when I get the pulling sensations, I fly to the furthest outreaches of our colony, gaze out into the distance, and remember what I have already done and seen. These little excursions are tolerated by everyone and they make the pain in that small part of my heart subside. But the rest of my heart, the largest part, is full. It is filled with the love and dedication to my wife, my children, my friends, and my colony. In other words; home. And that is more than enough for me.

BIOGRAPHY

 **Paul Vincent Rodriguez** was raised in the small town of Alma, Michigan. He spent a lot of time in the woods of the northern Lower Peninsula where nature had not yet been disturbed and where magical creatures prevail. It wasn't until he had children that he found that magic is everywhere—even in cities. It is his hope that someday, everyone will be able to see the magic too.

Coming Soon

TALES OF FAIRIES

The Tale of
Darvin
THE Nerd

TALES OF FAIRIES

The Tale of
Flaylen
THE Fallen

www.ingramcontent.com/pod-product-compliance
Lightning Source LLC
Chambersburg PA
CBHW021112130626
46554CB00002B/658

9780984328123